"Laura once again write[s ...] ing heartache, anxiety, [...] God reminds us that He w[ill never leave us and that we can do] things through Christ, who gives us strength."

— DANIELLE DARAH, communications and entrepreneurship undergraduate student, Miami University

"It's so easy to immerse yourself in this novel. The combination of emotion, familiarity, and faith captures your attention to a point where you feel as if you are Emma and that her anger is your anger, her struggles are your struggles, and her relief is your relief. To have such a simple and relatable story made my heart beat faster with each new and heart-wrenching scene and made me realize the true and genuine realism this book has to offer."

— OLIVIA KRAWCZYK, student at Miami University

"Laura L. Smith writes of a very familiar experience: life falling apart and falling back together with God's love and forgiveness."

— AMANDA TULLIS, Miami University student

"Laura Smith's books are about everyday life."

— BRIANNA NIXON, freshman, Talawanda High School

"*Angry* is compelling and heart-wrenching. Author Laura Smith grabs your attention and has it throughout the entirety of the book. As Emma goes through hard times, you feel for her as if it were you back in high school."

— KELCI HOUSE, photographer; photo editor for *Up Magazine*

DOWNLOAD
A FREE DISCUSSION GUIDE AT
www.NavPress.com

Angry

A NOVEL

LAURA L. SMITH

Discipleship Inside Out™

NavPress is the publishing ministry of The Navigators, an international Christian organization and leader in personal spiritual development. NavPress is committed to helping people grow spiritually and enjoy lives of meaning and hope through personal and group resources that are biblically rooted, culturally relevant, and highly practical.

**For a free catalog go to www.NavPress.com
or call 1.800.366.7788 in the United States or 1.800.839.4769 in Canada.**

© 2010 by Laura L. Smith

All rights reserved. No part of this publication may be reproduced in any form without written permission from NavPress, P.O. Box 35001, Colorado Springs, CO 80935. www.navpress.com

NAVPRESS and the NAVPRESS logo are registered trademarks of NavPress. Absence of ® in connection with marks of NavPress or other parties does not indicate an absence of registration of those marks.

ISBN-13: 978-1-60006-623-8

Cover design by Disciple Design
Cover images by iStockphoto, Getty Images, Shutterstock
Author photo by Kelci House

Musical and lyrics from *Les Misérables*, composed by Claude-Michel Schönberg and Alain Boublil; lyrics by Herbert Kretzmer, copyright © 1980. Based on novel Victor Hugo, *Les Misérables* (1862).

This novel is a work of fiction. Names, characters, places, and incidents are either the product of the author's imagination or are used fictitiously. Any resemblance to actual events, locales, organizations, or persons, living or dead, is entirely coincidental and beyond the intent of either the author or publisher.

Library of Congress Cataloging-in-Publication Data

Smith, Laura L., 1969-
 Angry : a novel / Laura L. Smith. -- 1st ed.
     p. cm.
 Summary: Emma resents babysitting for her five younger brothers and sisters, is angry that her parents are divorcing, and is frustrated with herself, until she finds strength in her belief in God and discovers that she is a talented singer.
  ISBN 978-1-60006-623-8
 [1. Singers--Fiction. 2. Family problems--Fiction. 3. High schools--Fiction. 4. Schools--Fiction. 5. Christian life--Fiction.] I. Title.
 PZ7.S6539An 2010
 [Fic]--dc22
                            2010016140

Printed in the United States of America

1 2 3 4 5 6 7 8 9 10 / 14 13 12 11 10

For my mom, who never gets angry but instead spreads God's love wherever she goes

Acknowledgments

THANK YOU...
To God, the author of all the plays enacted on the stage of life, for giving me the gift of words. Help me use them to always serve You.

To Brett for teaching me the lesson Jean Valjean had to learn for himself: "To love another person is to see the face of God!"

To Maddie, Max, Mallory, and Maguire for making my heart sing and my soul dance; as we cling to each other I feel entwined in love.

To Rebekah Guzman for expertly and exquisitely producing the stories God has put in my heart and for believing in Emma, Lindsey, Melissa, Raven, and Gracie enough to put their names up in lights, where they can share their stories with countless others.

To Amy Parker for all of your poignant, heartfelt stage directions, polishing my manuscript until it was worthy of its debut. I am blessed to call you my editor and friend.

To NavPress for being such a phenomenal crew, flawlessly handling all of the props, costumes, bookings, programs, tickets, lights, makeup, and sets for opening night.

To Marie and Ryan Steffen for allowing me backstage access to rehearsals of Talawanda High School's theatre department, giving me an insider's eye to the high school stage.

To Drew Campbell and Becca Hart for being my acting coaches. Your expertise in high school auditions, rehearsals, and productions was priceless.

To Tammy Bundy for rehearsing my lines with me until I was ready for the performance. You are an amazing cast mate!

Chapter One

The latest issue of *Lucky* is spread out in front of me. I'm checking out the three hot nail colors for fall and thinking I need to pick up a bottle in a gunmetal shade, which, they say, looks better on short nails. Ha! They're totally selling to us nubbynails. Then Peter walks by. He's so cute with his blonde buzz and wire-framed glasses, even though he is kind of pale. His buff, hockey bod is all exposed in his swimsuit. I catch my breath. My best friend in the world, Lindsey, elbows me.

"I'm not blind," I whisper.

"Are you going to talk to him?" Lindsey asks from beneath her black movie-star shades. Easy for her to ask. She is tiny, tan, and gorgeous, and *her* hockey player boyfriend is totally into her.

I have to wear 50 SPF; otherwise I'll look like a lobster. I have red hair and marshmallow-white skin. I don't actually tan — I just keep freckling and freckling until I have so many freckles they kind of blend together into a tannish color.

"Doubtful." I turn the page, trying to act like it's no big deal. But I feel all wiggly inside, like a bowl of orange Jell-O with mandarin oranges in it. I'm so pathetic. When Peter talks to me, I'm hypnotized. I do whatever he asks, which at times has been way more than I should do. We messed around a lot last school year. I was so into him — too into him. I don't know why. Maybe because it feels good to have someone pay attention to me. Maybe because it's a thrill. I even stayed out with him all night. At one point I thought I was pregnant. The good news: I wasn't pregnant. The bad news: my parents freaked, and I got grounded for the staying out part (they didn't know the might-be-pregnant part) for an entire month. When I couldn't go out for those four eternal weeks, Peter started seeing Elisa, some cutesy gymnast girl, *and* I wasn't allowed to try out for the spring play. Total screwup! Risk everything to be with him. Get caught. Get grounded. Lose a role and lose him. Life sucks sometimes.

"I'm getting in the water," Melissa says from the end of our row. "I'm melting." Melissa's on dance team with Lindsey. She's really sweet and kind of quiet and definitely naive. She's always agreeable and never judges any of us, which is a plus, but she's a little shaky at times.

"I'm with you, sistergirl," Raven chimes in. "Let's go off the board." Raven moved here from Atlanta two years ago. She plays soccer with Gracie. Gracie is Melissa's best friend from grade school, and that's how we all ended up friends. We just kind of landed together, and now we're inseparable.

Melissa stands and straightens the straps of her ultra-conservative, yellow tank suit.

Raven turns toward us. "Y'all coming?"

"I am." Gracie stands. Her simple black bikini looks striking with her jet black hair and pale olive skin. Her silver ankle bracelet is the only adornment on her elegant body. It looks great on her, but I would never go for that look. The brighter and bolder the better for me. My swimsuit has a leopard top and black bottoms. The band on the bottom is thick enough to cover some of my belly and the top is cut low enough to show some of my cleavage. Play to your assets. I baby-sat my younger brothers and sisters

ANGRY

a boatload of hours to pay for it, but it was completely worth it.

"I'll be there in a minute." Lindsey waves them on, pointing to her magazine.

"Go ahead." I tilt my head.

"So, you won't even talk to him anymore?" Lindsey quizzes me as soon as the rest of the gang heads for the high dive.

"It's useless. He likes Elisa."

"I heard she's dating Andrew Metzger."

When I was little I used to stick out my tongue whenever something didn't go my way or whenever I was frustrated. As I've matured, I've learned to keep my tongue inside my mouth, but I still have the reflex to stick it out. I push my tongue to the place where my braces used to rest on the inside of my bottom row of teeth and push that thought around in my head. *Does that mean he's available?*

"I don't know what to do with that information. I'd finally accepted the fact he's with someone else. I don't know if I can go there." I stare right into Lindsey's eyes.

"I know, sweetie." Lindsey places her tiny pink fingernails on my hand. "He's so stupid. C'mon, let's cool off."

Raven's athletic body arcs from the dive. I see a flash of her tangerine tank and matching board shorts as she splashes into the aqua pool.

I dive into the water. I need to wash off these Peter feelings.

Submerging myself in the water is like entering a dark, air-conditioned movie theatre in the heat of summer. Everything goes from light to dark, from hot to cold in an instant. I relish the severe change from the blistering world above to this aquatic one, where images are blurred and feelings are numbed. I long to be Ariel and swim off to my secret grotto. I linger below the surface as long as I can, until my lungs force me to come up for air.

I emerge, keeping my eyes closed as I inhale the thick, sweet air, perfumed with tropical suntan lotions, chlorine, and body heat.

Ummmmm. I savor the moment.

Lindsey sits on the edge of the pool. Her pedicured toes dangle in the water, but her petite body stays on land in its itsy-bitsy, teeny-weeny, yellow, lime, pink, and black color-blocked bikini.

Melissa swims over. "I think Beau's here!" she whispers to us, as if Robert Pattinson had just appeared.

"He's your boyfriend, Mel!" Lindsey puts her in line. "Why don't you grab your towel and go sit with him?"

Melissa squeezes her eyes tight. "Sure. Why not?" She pauses then squints her mossy green eyes. "I can't do that!"

"Sure, you can. I'll help." Lindsey looks to me for assistance.

I look to the clock to escape this ridiculous conversation. Melissa can be such a baby sometimes. She and Beau have been dating almost two years, and she can't go sit with him? I'd go sit with him, if I found him at all interesting.

It's five o'clock!

"Perfect!" I yell, clearly indicating things are everything but perfect. I was supposed to be home at five o'clock with corn on the cob from the farmer's market for dinner. One of the drawbacks of being ungrounded from the car: I'm expected to run corny family errands.

"What's up?" Lindsey asks. Melissa looks offended by my sarcasm. I pull myself from the clear, cool sanctuary of the water and roll my eyes at her.

"While you two girls take a daring promenade to the other side of the pool, I'm going to grab my stuff. I'm late, and Mom's gonna kill me!"

"Let me walk Mel over there, and I'll ride home with you." Lindsey stands.

"Then you've gotta be in high gear," I call back already halfway to our chairs. Lindsey's coaching Melissa. She touches her slightly on the arm and appears to be in the most engaging conversation of her life. I shake my head. Lindsey's incredible. She was born with that knack for seducing men, befriending girls, and getting everyone to be enamored with her. She doesn't get I'm on the fly.

I slide on my flip-flops, stuff my towel, magazine, and phone into my tote. I look up, don't see Lindsey, grab her stuff, and shove it into her bag. I should find Raven and Gracie and say good-bye, but Mom will scream at me as is. I dart toward the entrance, catch Lindsey's eye on the way, and wave her over to me.

"Here's your stuff. I am so in for a screamfest."

"Blame it on me." Lindsey takes her bag and walks with me. "Did you check out with Rav and Gray?"

"No." I shake my head and roll my eyes, like a chastised child.

"I'll text them in the car." She smiles. "Melissa and Beau are so cute. He was giddy she came over to talk to him. He was totally by himself, and like what boy comes to the pool alone right before dinner? He was so looking for her and an excuse to take her home." Lindsey laughs out loud.

I half-listen to Lindsey as she gabs on the way to the farmer's market and then to her house.

Lindsey checks herself in the visor mirror as I pull into her driveway. "Thanks for the ride, sweetie. See ya tomorrow." She grins as she crawls out of my hand-me-down Jetta. I roll my eyes at her. She's so chipper all the time.

I can't be all smiley when Peter totally ignored me, and I know Mom's waiting to ground me.

I park at the curb, grab my bag of corn, and dash into the house. Everything is oddly quiet for pre-dinnertime in our house.

With my five little brothers and sisters, it's usually pure chaos. I take the corn into the kitchen, cringing with anticipation at Mom's lecture, but she's not there. I hear Dad's phone voice coming from the screened-in porch. I head that way expecting one of my brothers or sisters to pop up like a ghost in a haunted house.

"No, no, that's great," Dad says in a sickeningly sweet tone. "Yeah, I'll meet you there. I can't wait." He speaks with the excitement of a kid, so unlike Dad. He's usually so rigid and firm, the epitome of the bank employee that he is—always wearing navy suits, speaking in calming tones that could soothe anyone with financial woes. "Oh, and I have a surprise for you."

I'm lured in. Who is he talking to? It's like the surprise sits in a wrapped package on the table in the middle of the porch for me to open. I walk out and for a split second Dad jerks his head. I must have startled him. He instantly returns to his nonchalance. "I have something new dreamed up for us." He nods at me and clicks shut his phone.

"Emma, when did you get home?" he asks.

"Just a second ago." I glance around for evidence of the surprise. "What's the surprise?"

"Surprise?" He looks puzzled. "Oh," Dad's dark eyes light up, and he chuckles, "It's nothing. Just a new game for the twins' soccer practice tomorrow. We're going to play a scrimmage with three balls on the field at once. They'll go crazy trying to figure out who should be where when. That was my assistant coach."

I scrunch my eyebrows. That's not exactly the kind of surprise that gets me excited, but I guess for a dad that would be a thrill.

"Emma, is that you?" Mom's irritated voice rubs me like sandpaper.

"Yeah, out here," I respond meekly.

Mom stomps out ready to roar, but Dad taps her on the head

ANGRY

with his briefcase and her scowl melts into a smile.

"Emma was out here running over my coaching strategy. Do you remember when I coached your team, Em? What were we called — the Good and Plentys? Remember those pink and black uniforms?"

I laugh. "I think we won two games all season."

Dad smiles, showing a few too many teeth, and turns to Mom, "And, if it weren't for your mother, we wouldn't have even won those two. Remember how you picked up Chloe, our best player, for both of those games, because she didn't have a ride?"

"Anything for the world of sports." Mom laughs, her anger dissolved by Dad's charm. She eyes me. "Did you get my corn?"

"Sure. I'll go husk it." I dart out, thankful to Dad for miraculously saving me from her wrath. I grab the bag, take it to the front porch, and start pulling rough husks and silky strands from yellow kernels.

Becca, my five-year-old sister, appears like one of the fairy godmothers she's infatuated with and asks, "Can I help?"

"Sure." I shrug.

Chapter Two

I wake up to the sound of someone sobbing. It's not Becca. It's too far away. It's not Billy. It's not his baby squawks. Is it Bennett, my seven-year-old brother? Or one of the twelve-year-old twins Hannah or Anna? I look at the clock: 4:55 a.m.! I squeeze my eyes closed. I cannot wake up this early. I physically cannot!

Uh-eheheheh! It almost sounds like Mom. The sobs are mature and muffled, but I'm exhausted and dazed. I climb down the ladder of my bunk and head toward the room Bennett shares with the twins. I put my ear to the door — silence, peaceful, magical silence — the kind only the Sandman can bring.

Sehwh, hahuhuhuh. The cries are definitely coming from Mom and Dad's room. I turn into a statue in the hallway at the sound of Dad's voice.

"Listen, Helen. I couldn't sleep, and I went out for a drive." Dad's voice, clear and matter-of-fact, wafts down the hallway. "How can you be so untrusting?"

"I know you were with *her*!"

"With who, Helen?" I can't see Dad, but I can picture him with his hands on his hips, shaking his head in disgust at Mom's exaggerated antics. "That's what I thought," he exhales. "You do whatever you need to. I'm going downstairs to try to catch a little sleep before the alarm goes off, and I have to go to work to pay for your house and your clothes and all the things your pathetic little business can't buy." Dad sounds like he's talking to a child. I hear him moving about. I should get back to my room, but my feet are glued to the floor. I can't move. The stairs lay between their room and me.

"I know you're lying!" Mom howls.

Mom loves to pick fights, but she usually has the upper hand. Now, she sounds sniveling. This is all too weird. I try to melt into the wall.

Dad's footsteps stomp down the stairs. Lucky for me, he didn't turn on the hall light or I would have been caught in the spotlight.

Mom whimpers in the darkness of her room. I can't go in there. I wasn't supposed to hear this. Is it even happening? Maybe it's all just a bad dream.

I creep back to my bunk bed. Becca kicked off her covers. I pull them back over her chubby legs. She looks so peaceful, unaffected by the things she didn't hear. I hunker down back into my sea of quilts and close my eyes.

I toss and turn. I kick all my old stuffed animals to the end of my bed. I need to go to the bathroom, but am afraid to walk down the hall and hear Mom crying or bump into Dad or something. What's going on? Is Dad really sleeping around? Come on! Dad? Who would want to sleep with him? Is Mom finally losing her mind? They fight all the time, but no one's ever mentioned *cheating* before. That's a heavy word. That could change everything.

I refuse to look at the clock. I try to count sheep. I get to forty-nine before I'm bored out of my skull. Who thought up that crazy exercise anyway? I rub my tongue across the backs of my teeth. Where would Dad have been driving? Did I hear them right? Everything's so hazy, I can't keep straight what I heard. I still have to pee.

The next thing I know, it is 7:45, and Billy's chattering away in his crib. I wonder how long he's been awake. I shake my head and blink at the sunlight streaming through the prism hanging from our window shade. Rainbows of light and color reflect on the walls of our room like fairy dust promising unexpected magic.

I hear the other kids playing. Sounds like Becca found her way into their room, and there's an elaborate game of make-believe occurring with her as the queen.

I scoop Billy from his sea of stuffed animals, and he burrows into my shoulder.

"I wuv woo," he says.

"I love you too," I whisper. I walk zombie-like to the bathroom, Billy in tow. I pee, finally. As I pop Billy's little bottom on the potty, my mind slowly returns to the awake world. It flashes to the middle of the night. Was that real? My heart thumps with anticipation. I wash Billy's and my hands in seconds flat, more like a quick rinse, and race toward Mom and Dad's room. What will I see? It's like watching *Friday the 13th* and covering my eyes, then peeking through them. I don't want to know what's going to happen next, but I can't stand to miss it either. But instead of Jason wearing a white hockey mask, the bed is made, the curtains are open, and the sun shines onto the burgundy floral comforter just like any other morning. The scent of Mom's perfume still tickles the air where she's moved around and left her impression on the room.

I head downstairs, clutching Billy. What will I see down here? Crumpled covers on the couch? Mom crying into her coffee? I'm afraid of what I'll find, but still holding out hope it was a dream. There's no evidence of Dad sleeping on the couch. Everything looks neat and orderly as it should be.

Mom's in the kitchen, slicing watermelon wedges and piling them on a huge tray.

"Good morning, Emma," she says, plopping a chunk of rind in her compost receptacle. Mom looks exactly how I'll look when I'm her age. Everyone tells us so, and although I outwardly deny any resemblance, we're so alike, it's almost scary. We both have this curly red hair, creamy skin covered in freckles, eyes reminiscent of a tiger's, a few extra pounds sitting on our hips, a love for bright colors, and tempers we can't control. Today she wears her hair pulled into a low ponytail with curly bangs falling to the side.

"Hey, Mom." I rub Billy's soft pj-ed back. "Where's Dad?"

"At work. You guys slept in this morning."

"Mom, are you okay?" I ask.

"I'm just on my way out the door and trying to get breakfast organized for you before I take off." She whisks the tray to the table without looking at me.

Mom owns a paint-your-own pottery store called The Magic Paintbrush. I baby-sit my brothers and sisters as a summer job. I'd way rather work in the store and paint cool picture frames for my friends and drawer pulls for my room, but that isn't the deal. It works out all right. I'm done every day by three and have all my weekends off. Plus, I don't have to wear a goofy uniform or sling burgers or anything. But I can't take any days off, and I always have to wake up early.

I swear Mom was sobbing last night. Should I let it go? This is so awkward. I don't want to call my mom a liar, but I should make sure she's okay. My whole body feels hot and prickly. "It's just I thought I heard you crying last night." I shift my weight. Billy rolls his heavy head onto my other shoulder.

"Me?" Mom opens the fridge and sticks her head inside.

ANGRY

"It must have been one of the little ones—a bad dream or something." She emerges holding a jug of milk. "Here, Billy. Mama will pour you some milk." She beeps him on the nose. Is she still averting my eyes?

"Oh," I say. Maybe I was dreaming. But, why won't she look at me, and if she wasn't crying, wouldn't she think it was odd that I *thought* she was?

"Gotta run. I have a birthday party for some eight-year-olds coming into the shop this morning." She walks toward me. I try to peek through her glasses to see if her eyes look red or puffy, but the rectangles obscure my view. She kisses Billy on the head. "See you, sport. Be good for EmEm."

She walks toward the garage. "I'll be home at three."

"Bye." I mumble. Should I have pushed her more? I didn't mention I heard her accuse Dad of being with someone else, or that he slept on the couch. I don't have any proof, but it all seemed so real. Should I let it go? It might be easier to let it go. I am so not willing to examine what all of this might mean. I feel like I have a mosquito bite on the bottom of my foot that itches like crazy, but I can't reach it. If I don't think about it, will it stop itching?

Chapter Three

"Anybody want anything?" I ask Lindsey, Raven, and Gracie as I stand to go toward the pool concession stand. Melissa wasn't feeling well today, so our group is one lawn chair short.

"I'd kill for a diet." Lindsey slides me a five. She always has extra cash. Her dad has some big-time job.

"I'm good." Raven smiles without taking out her earbuds.

As I walk across the scalding concrete, I float back into the parent scenarios that I've been playing through my head. As real as it seemed at the time, now, it's more like a movie I watched. I've been observing them all week, but they've been bizarrely calm. No arguments that I've seen. Dad's been working like crazy, and Mom's obsessed with her store, and my siblings fill in all the cracks.

There's just one person in front of me in line, Kate from my drama class. Kate is tall and stocky, not carrying around a few extra pounds like me, but strong, with wide shoulders — swimmer's shoulders. She's been on swim team since she was little. Her dark, glossy curls fall right below her shoulders, and her green eyes are darker than mine, a mossy color, almost brown.

"Hey."

"Hey, Emma," she says in her husky voice.

"How's your summer? I haven't seen you at all."

"Yeah, I had swim team every morning way early and then meets on weekends usually. I've been working for my dad a few hours in the day, and I had to go to bed early to be up for practice. It's finally over! I basically had no social life." Kate looks down at her flip-flops. Kate's personality kills me. She is quiet, practically silent in social settings, but on stage she's outrageous. She'll play any kind of character and do prat falls or curse or fake love scenes, anything. "But," she looks up and gives a sheepish smile, "I have newfound hope in my acting career." She takes her bottle of Vitamin Water from the kid behind the window, who I think is Isaac Greenberg's little brother.

"Oh, yeah?" I turn to the kid. "Nachos, extra jalapeños, and two Diet Cokes." It pains me that they don't carry Mountain Dew here.

"Aren't you going to ask me what it is?" Kate looks at me, her inner actress coming out at the topic of drama.

I hand the kid some cash. It's definitely Isaac's brother—I forget his name.

"What is it?" I chomp into a suspiciously stale chip. A dribble of warm, spicy cheese slides down my tongue.

"I heard Ricardo is putting on *Les Mis* in the fall."

"Get out!" I squeal. Ricardo Gomez is our drama teacher, and we've never done anything other than Rodgers and Hammerstein for our musicals. Plus we always do a play in the fall and our musicals in the spring. "Does he realize *Les Mis* came out in the last forty years? We don't even have the fly space for it!" I'm picturing the rotating stage and the enormous barricade of the *Les Misérables* set and trying to size it up on our school stage. Math is not my strong suit, but the geometry is simple enough to know it just won't fit.

"That's the rub. Rumor has it we'll perform at the community college's auditorium, and the only time they had it available was fall."

I'm bouncing up and down, I'm so excited. With my red hair, the character Fantine is a dream role of mine. I'd take any role, but could you imagine?!

"Who'd you hear it from?" I grip Kate's arm.

"I swore I wouldn't tell." Kate examines the pink liquid in her bottle. "But I would definitely call it a reliable source. Hey listen, I gotta go, but call me tonight." She pivots on her heel and walks away, her dark curls bouncing behind her back. She's clearly trying to intensify the mystique behind her piece of gossip.

I want to scream out loud. I try to walk like a normal person back to our chairs. Lindsey's sitting there all google-eyed at her boyfriend, Noah. Of course, she won't call him her boyfriend—anymore. She claims she's cooling things off with him, but they're still smitten with each other. I should probably wipe the drool off Noah's chin with my napkin. Imaginary horns blast the music for *Les Mis* in my ears.

Raven and Gracie must be in the pool. Their chairs sit vacant. Despite Lindsey and Noah's romantic interlude, I need to tell someone or I'm going to burst. I plop into my lawn chair, hand Lindsey her drink, and try to keep my voice below a scream. "You'll never believe it!"

"Believe what?" Lindsey asks.

Noah leans back. "Hey, Emma."

"Hi." I give a quick smile, even though he's totally ruining my announcement.

"Sounds like Ricardo is producing *Les Misérables* in the fall and that would be the most incredible, most fabulous production our high school has ever done. And I've seen it like six times, and I've wanted to be Fantine since I was a little girl!"

"I love that show. I bawled at the end." Lindsey sighs.

"Everyone bawls at the end!" I squeal. "That's the whole point! A show that evokes that kind of emotion from the audience!" I pop the lid of my drink. "I mean last year, they did *Oklahoma*, and it was cute and catchy, and everyone loves Ado Annie. But come on — nobody left all tangled up inside."

"Who's Ricardo?" Noah asks.

"Ricardo Gomez. He's the drama teacher." I take a sip of cool, bubbly sweetness.

"Oh, yeah, I know that guy." Noah nods.

"So, I take it you're going to audition." Lindsey's words are measured. She knows how bummed I was last year when I didn't make the fall play and then was grounded from trying out for the spring musical. But, junior year is going to be my year. I took both of Ricardo's drama classes last year to get to know him better and to hone my craft. This is where it all starts over again. This is my chance.

"Yeah." I nod. "I think it's about time."

"So, when are tryouts?" Noah asks.

"I don't know," — I chug another swallow of Diet Coke — "but I'm going to find out."

"I've gotta get goin'." Noah smiles at Lindsey, grabs his towel, and stands. "Hey, ladies, I'm having a big party at the Freezer for my eighteenth in two weeks. You should come." He tears his eyes away from Lindsey for a second and looks at me. "Really, both of you. It should be really cool." He laughs in his deep, rolling laugh at his pun.

"That would be great! Wouldn't it, Em?" Lindsey cheers. "I can't skate very well, though."

"There will be music and pizza and stuff too. You don't have to be on the ice the whole time. You have to come." Noah winks at Lindsey.

ANGRY

"Keep me posted on auditions, Emma."

"Thanks. I'll post it on Facebook if I get a part." He really is a nice guy. I just get annoyed with all the drama between him and Lindsey sometimes. Broken up? Right!

He leans down and puts his hand on Lindsey's thigh, slick with sunscreen. "See ya."

"I'll walk out with you." She stands.

Surprise, surprise.

I dig in my bag for my iPhone and slip in my earbuds. I scroll to the *Les Mis* soundtrack. I wonder what song Ricardo will have us sing for auditions. I lean back, letting the sun ooze into my skin while the melodies of the French Revolution sashay between my ears.

Chapter Four

"Come on, Emma," Hannah calls. "We're gonna be late."

"You're late for everything else you do in life. Why should soccer practice be any different?" I ask, scanning the counter for my car keys.

"But we like to get there early to kick the ball around with Dad, and soccer's important." She shakes her head at me for not realizing the whole world revolves around her shin guards.

"I grabbed your water bottle," Anna says, tossing the red bottle to her double. They both wear their hair in bobs, just long enough so they can pull it back in ponytails, which they do almost every day, with thin headbands pulling back any stray, red hairs. They are thin as rails; apparently they got Dad's body type, and have his dark chocolate eyes. They look so much alike they love to trick their teachers, friends, and teammates. They can never trick me, even though they've tried. Hannah has a little dimple on her right cheek, and Anna's eyebrows arch higher than Hannah's.

"Go ahead and get in the car," I say. "I need to find my keys."

"I think I saw them on our bathroom counter," Hannah says.

I run up the stairs, swipe them in my hand, and see Billy march past with a plastic firefighter's hat on.

"I being fie fie," he declares.

"Go put out a fire, buddy!" I cheer him on.

"Mom, I'm taking the twins to practice," I call down the hall.

"Thanks, Emma." She emerges from her bedroom, wearing a really cool top I haven't seen before.

"Great top, Mom." I wonder how many times she has to wear it before I can borrow it.

"Thanks." Despite the cool shirt, Mom looks crummy, like she hasn't slept in days. I better look into some good skin cream, so I don't end up looking that old in my forties.

"Billy just ran into my room to put out a fire. See ya."

"Bye." Mom follows Billy's invisible trail into my room.

Even though Dad's the coach, he doesn't drive the twins to practice because he always comes straight from work. He must change into his T-shirt and shorts in the car or a phone booth like Superman or something. Part of the price I pay for being able to drive is to transport the rest of the family too. So, I drop the twins off and pick up stuff Mom needs from the store. But I don't have to worry about picking up the twins. They ride home with Dad.

As I pull into the parking lot at the field, I see Dad's car is there. He's standing next to the goal with Carol, who is Jennifer's mom and his assistant coach. Three of the twins' teammates are already passing the ball to one another in a triangle while they wait for practice to officially start.

"There you go, guys," I say as I put the car in park.

"Thanks, Em," Hannah says, opening the door.

"Yeah, thanks, Em," Anna echoes, grabbing the straps of her soccer bag.

"Have fun," I call.

I watch them run over to the field. They're so excited to see Dad—just like I used to be when he coached me. It felt so special to be the coach's daughter. He pushed me hard, but he also made me feel special by giving me the inside scoop, like helping him put together the lineups or telling me where all the teams we played ranked in the league.

He laughs and tilts his head back as he chats with Carol. He's got such an ease about him. A little more relaxed than his usual banker man role. Could there really be "another woman"? I still can't figure out if the argument with my folks happened, or if it was a nightmare. I can't get it out of my head. But why would I dream Mom to be so forlorn? Where would Dad meet someone? When would he date her? He's so busy; he couldn't possibly have time to see someone else. But there was that weird phone call on the porch. He said it was soccer. I don't know. My imagination tends to run wild.

Dad doesn't see the twins coming, but they're charging from behind at different angles. They're coconspirators in everything. They collide into him at the exact same moment. He wobbles, but doesn't fall.

He turns around and laughs when he sees Hannah and Anna. He roughs their heads and sends them out with the other girls.

Kate's texting me.

Auditions next week. Can I have a ride?

I text back.

Deal. Dust off your dancing shoes.

The rumors are true! Kate fills me in on all the details and auditions are on Monday. My throat feels all tickly. I tap my fingers on the steering wheel. I'm supposed to grab milk, dishwasher liquid, and Doritos for Mom on the way home, which I could get at the grocery. But if I go to Target, I can get a new pair of tights too. I need a new pair of black tights to audition in. All my old ones have runs. I could look for a new tank too — something eye-popping bright, so that I'll stand out. Green's my best color. If they have an emerald green tank or leotard, I'm buying it too.

My old character shoes will have to do. Foot undies are out of the question. They're all the rage — little strappy things you wear on your feet to dance. It's almost like going barefoot, thus their name. But I don't have enough cash for tights, a tank, and shoes. Plus, there's really nothing wrong with my old shoes; they're just scuffed. I'll use some of Dad's shoe polish to cover up the scuffs.

Chapter Five

After dinner I brave underneath my bed in search of my character shoes. I find some old Pokemon cards I used to collect, two CDs I'd written off as lost, one of my favorite bracelets, a couple of earring backs, as well as countless magazines and a heap of dirty (at least they're dirty now) clothes. Finally, I uncover my shoes. I cradle them like Becca holds her baby dolls.

In the hall closet I find a clean washcloth and get it damp in the sink. Lovingly, I wipe the sides of the shoes as if they were Billy's sweet face. I carefully dry them with a bumpy towel, so as not to ruin the leather. I lay them on the counter and step back. Overall they look pretty good. From a distance they're fine, but as I take a step closer I see scuffs on the heels and cracking along the tops where my feet bend to do step-ball-changes.

I go into Mom and Dad's closet. All of her stuff is on the right, and all of his stuff is on the left. In the back corner is where Dad keeps an old shoe box filled with polish and rags. I can almost smell the intoxicating scent of shoe polish. It evokes memories of when I was little, and I watched him shine his shoes every Sunday night before a new work week. Dad makes more money now, and if his shoes get torn up he buys new ones. But every once in a while he'll still buff out a spot or clean up shoes that got splattered on a rainy day. It fascinated me how he could take a torn-up spot and make it look brand new.

I spot the familiar aqua and tan box, but stacked neatly under it is another plain white shoe box. I remove the lid from the polish box and smile at the familiar smell. I poke around for black, pure black to transform my shoes and grab a rag to buff them.

In my bathroom I spread out one of the old magazines I uncovered under my bed and work my shoes until they look worthy of Broadway, well almost. I'm the antithesis of a neat freak, but somehow I take pride in creating a flawless patina on my shoes. These shoes represent the high of performing—of twirling across wooden floors and filling high ceilings with my voice, pretending I am anyone who I am not.

When I'm finished I carefully replace the lid on the shoe polish and fold up the rag. I place them back in Dad's box exactly where I found them. He's so neat and orderly. He'd freak if anything were out of place, which makes me wonder about this white shoe box. I don't remember it ever being there. His shoe-shining supplies were always wedged in the back corner like a puzzle piece filling the right angle. Someone must have hastily plopped it on this white box.

I open the lid to see where this pair of shoes belongs—on the left or the right. But glancing at the contents, I know it couldn't even belong in our house, let alone in Mom and Dad's closet. On top is a picture of Carol, the twins' assistant coach, in a bikini at a beach somewhere. It almost looks like it came from her family album, except she's posed like a spread from *Sports Illustrated*, with her head tossed back and her legs bent just so. *This is so weird. How did it get here?* I lift the picture for an inkling of what to do with this box. I find a letter in someone's handwriting I don't recognize.

ANGRY

Just a reminder of our escape from the world. I'm thinking about you now and the things we did there and can't wait to do them with you again.

C

What in the world? The "C" must be for Carol. I feel like I'm a voyeur in Carol's—what's her last name anyway?—life. How did we get this box of her personal things?

"What do you think you're doing?" When Dad is angry, he frightens me. His voice is deep and stern, but freaky calm like Ed Norton in any of the movies where he's played the creepy guy.

"I, I . . ." I don't even know how to answer. I have no idea what I'm doing. I have no idea why these things are here, how they got in my hands, in our house, in their closet. I have no idea why Dad's voice implies he's ready to slap me across the face.

"I borrowed some of your shoe polish." I return the white lid that's still in my left hand on top of the mystery box. "I'm sorry, I should have asked." I feel unexplainably nauseous, like I've been caught committing the worst possible crime, only I don't know what it is.

Dad's brown eyes shine with a fire from somewhere deep within. I would back out of the room if I weren't trapped in the dead end of the closet.

"Why are you snooping?"

"I, wasn't . . . didn't mean to . . . don't know? I was putting back your shoe polish and this box"—I look at it like it's a troll in my hands—"it was under your box and you don't keep your box on top of anything." My voice shakes. Dad's not speaking, just glaring. I don't know what I've done wrong, but I know that box wasn't for me to see. It's someone else's personal things. Why is Dad so ticked?

"Hand me the box!"

I timidly scoot just enough forward to have the box make contact with Dad's hand, and quickly retreat back to my corner.

"It's so strange, Dad," the heat of saltwater brims in my eyes, but I don't know why I'm crying. "It's not ours."

"If it's not yours, you shouldn't be looking at it." If Snow White's evil stepmother had been a man, he would have spoken just like this and had the same sneer. Dad takes two steps backward, maintaining his burning gaze to clear the exit from the closet.

I scurry past him, hoping he doesn't throw the box at me or force-feed me a poison apple. He looks like he could eat me alive. I withdraw to my room, close the door, and collapse on my bed. The tears burn my cheeks. I didn't do anything wrong. I swear I didn't do anything wrong, but I feel like I just stole money from his wallet.

I stay in my room all night. No one seems to notice. No one comes to check on me. What horrible thing have I done? I feel like I personally lifted the lid to Pandora's Box.

Chapter Six

I'm in a fog as I lift Billy from his crib, remove his Pull-Up, exchange it for undies, and carry him downstairs. Somewhere in the shuffle Becca and Bennett join us like the children of Hamelin following the Pied Piper. I turn on the Disney channel. The twins are still sleeping, and I'm not sure where Mom is. I take advantage of everyone's enchantment with *Mickey Mouse Clubhouse*. I go to the bathroom and brush the heinous hairy taste out of my mouth. I pull on jean shorts and a neon orange tank. I bump into Mom in the hall.

"Is everyone up?" she asks in a whisper.

Mom's dressed for work and has makeup on, kind of, but she looks awful, like that time I got bit by a spider under my eye and my whole face swelled. I can't tell why she's all red and swollen. I don't mean to stare, but something's really not right.

"Mom, you okay?"

"No." She shakes her head. "I'm definitely not okay, Emma." She looks away and scrunches up her face.

"Mom?"

"I need to talk to you guys." She attempts to clear her throat. "Can you let me know when everyone's awake?"

I nod. My heart contracts. My whole chest feels tight. This is all wrong. Moms aren't supposed to say *they're* not okay. They're supposed to always be okay. What's wrong?

"G'morning," Hannah says groggily from behind.

"*Oaaahhhhyy.*" I turn to see Anna yawning beside her in her identical pink pajamas covered with monkeys.

"We're all up now."

I can hear Mom's lecture already about how messy the house is, how we're not pitching in enough around here, can't we see she works, blah, blah, blah. . . . I dare her with my eyes to say something upsetting. Whenever something gets to her, she takes it out on us. She's so extreme.

"Where are the little ones?" A foreign voice escapes Mom's lips.

"Downstairs." I lead the way. The twins wearily shuffle behind, and Mom takes the rear. As soon as we're all gathered in the family room, she clicks off the TV.

Becca, Bennett, and Billy moan in unison, "Aaaaahhh!"

The twins sit on the couch. Sensing danger, I instinctively gather Billy in my arms and stand behind the couch, waiting. I know I'm squinting.

Mom licks her top lip, looks down, looks up, squeezes her eyes shut, shakes her head, and lets out a nervous laugh.

"I practiced this, so I could get it right. And now . . ." She shakes her head again. Tears drop from her eyes as she opens her mouth. "Your father and I are getting a divorce." Her voice cracks on the word divorce, like she's on stage and her microphone has just gone out.

Bennett digs at a hole in his oversized Ohio State jersey. The twins are too tired to respond. Billy has a sudden urge to be free and wiggles out of my arms to the floor.

"But I don't want you to be diborced," Becca whines.

"What?" I finally manage to speak. Now my mouth is open,

ANGRY

it's not going to stop. I swear at my mom and follow with the question on all of our minds, "Why would you do that to us? To Dad?"

Mom's face turns scarlet. She stands there in front of the TV, like she is the TV. If this were a show, it would be the worst show I'd ever seen! I wish I had a clicker and could change the channel. "You will not speak to me like that, young lady!" she shrieks. "I am not doing this to you! Your father is doing this to you — to me — to all of us!"

Becca starts to cry. The hole in Bennett's jersey grows by the moment.

"Mommy," Hannah asks, sobbing, "what did we do wrong?"

Mom collapses onto the couch. She wraps one arm around Becca and rubs Hannah's leg with her free hand. Her voice catches again. "Dad's seeing someone else."

The blood in my veins is liquid fire. The hinge of my jaw aches. How can she say that? What is she saying? The memory of the white shoebox burns the palms of my hands. The way Dad tossed back his head at practice, the call on the porch, that night — it wasn't a bad dream. It was real. This is the nightmare.

"Go to hell!" I scream at no one in particular and everyone at once. I grab my keys and bolt. Sitting in the driver's seat, my hands shake so much, I can barely get the key in the ignition. I back out of the driveway and aim too far to the right, putting skid marks on the shrubs lining the driveway. I keep going.

I drive to the lake at the edge of town. I thrust the gear into park and let my head fall on the steering wheel. I bang my head again and again until my entire body shakes. I feel a tunnel inside of me cold, metallic; it is filled with pain, wretched pain that slides down to the bottom of the tunnel near my bellybutton and back up to the top of the tunnel near my throat. I don't feel individual tears fall, but somehow my entire face is soaked. I cry for an infinite amount of time. I don't have thoughts, just gut-wrenching pain. I can't allow myself to think. That would hurt more.

When I've cried what must be all the emotions I've ever possessed out of me, I lean back into my seat. I find some napkins in the glove box, wipe off my slimy face, and blow my nose. I grab the sweatshirt wadded up on the floor of the backseat and pull it over my head, then grab a piece of gum.

The sharp cinnamon wakes me from my divorce stupor. *Divorce!* Is that the word she used? Mom didn't say, "Dad and I are fighting." Or, "Dad and I are getting separated." Or, "I think Dad's having an affair." But, he is. He actually is. And it's with that Carol lady. Soccer season started only two weeks ago. How much could have happened? That's not long enough for them to have had a fling and her to go to the beach and miss him. None of it makes sense! It doesn't add up! No wonder he was livid when I found that box! And I felt miserable about it! He let me take the fall—made me feel like I'd betrayed him by being in his closet! What a jerk! What a first-rate, total, and complete jerk! I punch the console so hard I hurt my fist.

I have to get out of the car. I feel like I'm being smothered in here. I climb out and slam the door shut as hard as I can. It bounces back at me, as if it's mocking me, trying to hit me back. I jump to avoid getting battered by a door, and I curse at it! Is the whole world against me?

I lope over to a grassy spot on the hill and plunk to the ground. From here I can see sailboats sliding silently across the dark water. Ducks gather under picnic tables closer to the water's edge, searching for leftover crumbs.

I grab at pieces of grass, wet from the morning dew, and twirl them in my fingers, twisting them, tying their slippery strands

ANGRY

into knots and braids. Meanwhile my brain mulls over the scenes I don't want to see: Dad laughing with Carol, Carol in a swimsuit, Dad smiling on the porch, Mom's puffy eyes, Mom's sobs in the middle of the night. How could he?! How could she let him?! I pull on my grass chain until it snaps.

Cigarette smoke drifts in my nostrils from the nearby fishermen who sit under the bridge.

"People up here have lungs!" I yell. My voice gets swallowed by the air, so big and endless around me.

They always fight—about us kids, about who's responsible for what, about the house, about money. They always fight about The Magic Paintbrush—about how it makes Mom late and stressed and. . . . The forlorn honk of geese echoes above me as a flock flies above in a perfect V formation.

I hate them both! How can they do this? How can they do this to me?

Tears pour out again, covering my face in confusion and anger.

God, how can this be happening? How can You let this happen? What did I do to deserve this? You're bigger than this. You're God. You can stop this from happening!

I haven't talked to God in a while. I've basically had a super crappy year and haven't felt Him around much. I don't know why I even bothered to call out to Him now. He doesn't seem to care at all about my house full of redheads. Desperate times.

I dare Him, *Where are You God? Do You see everything? If You do, why are You letting this happen?*

Chapter Seven

When I run out of tears and can't bear to think for another moment, I stand up and get back in the car. Just like that. Like everything is normal. Only, everything's not normal. I have no idea how long I sat on the hill—hours, minutes? I was in such a rage when I stormed out of the house, I didn't even grab my phone, and the clock in my car was busted when I got it.

I drive on autopilot to Lindsey's. I park in her driveway. I can't see any lights through the leaded windows that frame the door. She has to be home. I don't know where else I'd go. I ring the doorbell and its chimes echo through the Kraus's enormous house. My stomach feels like it's been stretched back and forth, back and forth like a balloon someone's about to blow up. "Please be home, Lindsey." I can't go home. Not now. Maybe not ever.

"Em?" Lindsey's baby doll face peeks through a crack in the door.

"Can I come in?"

"Sure." Lindsey turns from the door and shuffles away in her boxers and cami. She plops on the couch in her family room and hugs a large, red, velvet throw pillow.

"What's up?" she asks. Her hair is sticking out in every direction, and she isn't wearing a trace of makeup. Even in this state, she can't help but look great. Sometimes she bugs me with her perfection.

"Did I wake you up?"

Lindsey raises her eyebrows. "Uh, yeah. It's like nine thirty in the morning."

"Sorry," I say halfheartedly, "I feel like I've been awake for weeks." The tears come again. I hate them. I wipe them crossly from the corners of my eyes with the back of my hand.

Lindsey gets up from her nest and sits next to me on the loveseat. She rests her forehead on mine and whispers, "Em, what is it?" Lindsey sobbed on my shoulder when her sister got caught smoking pot, and she's the only one in the world who understands how much I love my brothers and sisters. I'm probably the only one who remembers she used to have glasses and braces. She was there when I took the pregnancy test last year too. We've been through it all. I know she'll be here for me, but we've never had anything like this.

"My folks," I choke on the words, "they're, they're—" I can't finish. I bounce my knee, trying to bounce my tears back into my head.

"They're what?" Lindsey asks.

"Divorce." I force out the word. It's followed by a cascade of sobs.

Lindsey wraps her arms around me and holds me. "Seriously?" Her eyes fill.

I nod.

Lindsey starts to cry too. For a flash I'm angry she would dare to cry about this. She doesn't know how much this hurts. Then I realize she's crying for me. What would I do without Linds? We sit, sniffling together until I can breathe again. I pull away, feeling a bit babyish, having Lindsey hold me.

"Mom told us this morning." I shake my head. "We woke up, and she just announced it, like she was announcing what she was making for dinner or something."

"Why?" Lindsey asks. "I mean, I know they fight a lot."

"Dad's cheating."

"Sick. Really?"

"Super sick. She coaches the twins with Dad. Can you believe that? I mean what is she thinking? She clearly knows he's married and has kids." I search for the sharp edge of the tooth that refused to straighten with braces and jab my tongue on its crag. "Plus, it's my dad! Who would want to hook up with him? I can barely picture Mom with him, let alone some random."

"What is *he* thinking, Em? *He's* the one who's married and has kids. Is she married too? Are you sure something's going on?"

"I hadn't even thought about *her* being married." I shake my head. The whole thing is so disgusting. "I have no idea. I just know her name's Carol something and her daughter, Jennifer, is on the twins' team. They just started practicing a couple of weeks ago. I don't even know their last name." I lean back into the cushions, trying to fit the puzzle pieces together. "I heard him talking to her on the phone one night, and I found this box with a picture and a note. . . . There was more stuff in it, only I didn't see, because Dad caught me looking at it."

"No way! What did he do?"

"He completely freaked out and made me feel like an idiot." I roll my eyes. "Like it's my fault he's having an affair. Uuuuh!" I stamp my foot. "Plus, Mom's a piece of work too. She totally works all the time even though she knows he doesn't want her to."

Lindsey nods like she's waiting for me to say something else.

"Anyway, I completely blew a gasket and flew out of there. Maybe I shouldn't have left, but what did Mom expect me to do? Say, 'Aw, shucks, Mom. Too bad, have a nice day while I baby-sit'?"

"I can't believe this is happening," Lindsey whispers. "I mean, I feel like we're sisters, and I am so sorry."

"Me too," I whisper, and again the hot tears slide down my cheeks.

We sit for a while. I don't know where Lindsey's thoughts drift, but mine drift back to all the fights, to Mom's yelling and begging, and Dad's belittling and repulsion.

Lindsey's hand is on my arm. "Hey, Em?"

"Hmmmm?"

"I hate to do this, but I have to get to work. I'm supposed to be at the mall at eleven, in forty-five minutes, and I haven't showered yet. You want to come up and talk to me while I get ready?" Lindsey works at a hip shoe store at the mall. She barely gets paid anything and only works two or three shifts a week, but scores a sweet discount, which is the whole purpose of her working there.

"No. I've gotta go." I have to use every ounce of strength I have to stand. "Knowing Mom, she left everyone home by themselves."

"Love you," Lindsey says, hugging me. Our wet cheeks, now cool from their dampness, touch. "I'll call you after work and see how you're doing."

"Love you too. Thanks."

I creep back to my car, slightly stronger after seeing Lindsey, but still terrified of going home. Yet, I feel oddly magnetized to the scene of the crime.

I open the front door and find the house eerily quiet. I kick off my flip-flops. No one's downstairs. I peek in the garage. Mom's car is still here. At least she didn't leave the kids alone, but I'm so not in the mood to see her again. I head toward the stairs and step on something reminiscence of thorns.

"For crying out loud!" I screech. I double over, ready to pull spikes from my foot, only to find a lone Lego stuck to my instep.

ANGRY

I hurl the Lego against the wall, hoping for a release of my anger. But it's teeny and barely makes a sound. I spy a small mound of the building blocks on the corner of the carpet. I scoop a handful and throw them against the wall of the steps. They rat-a-tat like tap shoes on a wooden floor. I let myself fall amidst the rainbow of plastic pieces and bite my lip.

Chapter Eight

Dad didn't come home from work last night. I guess he got the message about the divorce.

This whole morning seemed like I was walking around in a fog. Mom left for work, like it was any normal day. She didn't say a word about my disappearing act yesterday. I let everyone watch *Scooby-Doo* DVDs while I got caught up on Facebook. On Bennett's request, we play a game of Twister in the family room. I read Billy and Becca a couple of picture books about mice. I make peanut butter and jellies for an early lunch, but I've run out of ideas. I've gotta get out of the house, or I'll go crazy. I feel like I'm trapped backstage after a show, the lights are out. Props litter the floor, making it easy to trip, and everyone's gone home. I need to see my friends. I need to escape this place where it all happened—where Mom and Dad fought, where Mom announced the divorce, where Dad left.

My friends will be at the pool. I guess that means packing the pool bag and the swim diapers and the rafts and taking the whole gang. Of course, it's exceedingly uncool to show up with all my little sisters and brothers, but the alternative is to spend today cooped up in this house wondering what else is in Dad's closet and cringing at the thought of one of my siblings asking me about the divorce. If I keep them busy, maybe none of us will have to deal with it.

We find a grassy area near the baby pool to set up shop.

"Here's the deal, guys," I tell them. "We're staying for three hours. If you're a big help, you can all get a snack. You decide when you get it. It doesn't matter to me. There's money in the pocket of the pool bag. Just take it up to the snack shack when you're ready."

"How much do M&M's cost?" Anna asks.

"A dollar fifty," Bennett answers matter-of-factly. He has a photographic memory, especially when it comes to numbers.

I line them up like soldiers awaiting inspection and spray them with sunscreen. There's no option for us fair-skinned, red-heads, other than to shield ourselves with 50 SPF.

"Owww! Owww! Owww!" Bennett wails.

"Oh, Ben!" I hold my brother close. I accidentally got spray in his eye. "I hate this stupid stuff." I throw the can down. "Are you okay?"

"It really hurts!" he whines with his eyes squeezed shut.

"I know." I shake my head. "I'm sorry." He's whimpering and people are staring. I need him to get quiet and go play and fast. "Tell you what, Ben," I take a towel and rub his closed eye to get any residue off his eyelid. "You can get an extra snack right now."

"Really?" He half opens his eyes to a squint, proving he hasn't actually been blinded.

"Really," I say, relieved that he's done crying and I haven't done any permanent damage to his cornea.

"Me too!" Becca cheers.

I exhale. Mom will kill me if we spend a fortune on snacks. Who cares? I get a sick kind of thrill out of her getting angry. I picture her opening the envelope where she keeps money for me to spend on the kids when we need it. A sneaky smile curls across my lips. "You too."

The twins eye me. I nod at them.

"Me too, me too, me too," Billy chirps.

"I would never forget you." I laugh and rub Billy's fluffy head. "Bennett, will you get Billy a Popsicle?"

"Sure."

That'll make everyone but Billy scarce for a little bit, and just in time. Here come the girls!

"Emma, I'm so sorry," Gracie says, hugging me.

"It's okay. Whatever." I shrug.

Melissa's right behind her. "Are you all right?"

"Of course not."

They arrange their towels as I vroom a truck in the grass with Billy.

Raven pulls a bag of Doritos from her tote. "I brought therapy."

I look up from the plastic Tonka. "Cool Ranch! My favorite!" I snatch the bag from her. "Thanks, Rav!"

A puff of spicy seasonings hits me in the face as I pull open the sides of the bag.

"If you need real therapy, you could always talk to my mom . . . or someone else in her office. Seriously, Em, it might be good to see a professional counselor about all of this." Lindsey shakes out a towel.

Bennett zips by and hands Billy an enormous rainbow swirled Popsicle and takes off for the boards. I decide to run interference and dodge Lindsey's suggestion. "Here, Billy, let Emma get the wrapper off for you. Remember how you're supposed to hold onto the stick and not the cold part?" Every once in a while brothers come in handy.

Randy, Raven's brother, spreads out his towel next to mine. "I'm going to sit with all you fine ladies. You make me look good."

He puts his arm around me. I know he's completely playing it up for me, but it does make me feel a little better.

We spend the day talking about everything from the affair my dad is having to the affair Angelina Jolie might be having. We evaluate the proof and speculate on the innuendo. We discuss what clothes we absolutely need for back to school. Raven and Gracie moan about how many laps they've been running at soccer practice, and everyone listens as I debate whether the twins should stay on their soccer team where Dad and this Carol person are their coaches.

Even though it means being ankle deep in chlorinated pee, my friends take turns playing with Billy in the baby pool. Raven starts a game of sharks and minnows with the twins and Bennett in the shallow end, and Melissa French braids Becca's hair.

When my charges are hot and tired and asking for a third snack, I decide to call it a day.

"See ya," I call to my girls. What would I do without them?

"Bring everyone back tomorrow," Lindsey calls.

"Just what you want"—I roll my eyes—"to be summer camp counselors."

"It'll give me an excuse to play Marco Polo," Raven chimes in.

"All right, just for you, Rav." I scoop Billy up with one arm and grab my pool bag with the other.

"Don't worry, sis, I'll play with you!" Randy pushes Raven into the pool. He doubles over laughing.

She pops up, grinning, pulls herself out of the pool, and points at Randy. "You'll pay, dear brother. You'll pay."

"Hannah, Anna, you guys grab the towels?"

"Got 'em," they say in unison.

"Emma," Gracie puts her hand on my shoulder and whispers, "I'm really sorry about everything with your parents, but at least you're sixteen. I mean, can you imagine if you were little like Billy or Becca? It must be horrible for them."

I feel like Gracie's punched me in the stomach. It's like she's my friend and thinks she's saying something nice, but her words are hideous.

"I don't think it matters how old you are!" I spit out the words as I swallow a lump the size of a stage light that's caught in my throat. "It's pretty crappy for me too!"

I turn my back before anyone sees the pools in my eyes and wave backward to the gang in general. "Outta here!"

I eventually get everyone buckled and all the doors to Mom's van closed.

"I have to go potty!" Becca announces.

We live less than five minutes away. "Just hold it." I bark.

I replay Gracie's comment as we turn into the neighborhood. Even a fun afternoon has to get spoiled for me. Just when I can't imagine anything more hideous happening, I spy Dad's truck in our driveway. I see it the second we turn onto the street. I feel Cool Ranch Doritos flipping and churning in my stomach. I blink and just sit there with my foot on the brake. What is he doing home? What are we supposed to do? Act normal? Drive around the block a couple of times?

"I'm gonna pee my pants!" Becca squirms.

"Hang on a minute." I have no choice. I pull into the driveway, past Dad's truck and into Mom's side of the garage. I unbuckle Becca, so she can scamper into the house. I get Billy out of his car seat and make sure the other three are out of Mom's van before I head inside. We trade cars when she works, so I have something big enough to haul the crew.

Dad emerges from the garage door wearing navy suit pants, a white and blue pinstriped shirt, and a bright red tie with small blue speckles. He's carrying an enormous brown cardboard box.

"I guess you heard Mom's kicking me out?" He laughs as if that's some kind of joke.

"Da-deeee!" Billy exclaims, oblivious to the severity of Dad's words.

Dad rubs Billy's puff of pumpkin hair. "Hey champ!"

"Where are you going?" I ask, not sure how to respond to his question.

"I'm staying with a friend for now," Dad answers and shifts his weight. "Let me get this loaded before I drop it." He continues toward the driveway.

With a friend? If it was one of his buddies, why doesn't he say "with Mike" or "with Scott"? I won't let him off this easily.

"You're staying with *her*, aren't you?" I screech.

"I want down," Billy demands. I lower him carefully to the ground.

"With who?" Dad says, as he bends over to brush a speck of dust off his shiny wingtip.

"With Carol." I dare him to deny it.

"Carol has been a good friend to me through all of this." He stands and walks back inside as if he's on a deadline to get his car loaded.

"So it's true?" I whisper as he emerges with another load.

"Your mother wanted it this way." Dad manages to slide his hand on my shoulder as he zips by with his roller bag.

Who would want anything this way?

"I made it!" Becca announces, peeking her enormous green eyes out the door.

"Hey, sweet pea," Dad calls, "have you been swimming?"

"Look at my hair!" She twirls for him to see her French braids.

"Very nice," he compliments. Then he turns back to me. "Tell

ANGRY

Mom I'll get the rest of it tomorrow. I'll call you." He kisses me, Bennett, and the twins one-by-one on our foreheads and climbs in his spotless truck. Like it's that easy. Like I'm delivering Mom a phone message, and like he'll call on the way home from work. Does he realize what's going on? I want to shake him until his tie flaps like a birds wings!

Becca runs after his truck. "Daddy, daddy, wait! Where are you going?"

"Wake up!" I scream. Does he see how *not* normal this is? Does he see Becca's tiny heart breaking? Does he see me standing here surrounded by everyone and their questions without any answers? But his windows are up, drowning out our pleas.

Chapter Nine

Three weeks before school starts. I whisk around the house humming one of Fantine's solos, "Hmmm, hmmm, hmmm, hmm-hmm, the light is fading..."

I pull on my black footless fishnets carefully, so I don't get a run. I don't know how my thunder thighs will squish into the netting, but fishnets are magical, like everything else about the theatre. Once they're on, they transform me from chubby Emma into sexy stage siren. That's what I love about being on stage; I can transform myself into anyone, into everyone, into someone who isn't me. I pull black athletic shorts over the tights. They cover my big rear, and supposedly black is slimming. The little slits up the side show just an extra hint of fish net. The tank I bought is perfect. Emerald green makes me feel like a queen. My black character shoes look new from a distance — from where the judges will be sitting. My thumb slides over one of the scuffs covered with black polish. I think of Dad's closet and the white shoe box.

"Not now!" I chastise the thought. "Today is my day." I strap on the shoes and sneak into Billy's room where a full-length mirror hangs on the back of his door. I take my dark kohl liner and outline my eyes. I coat my lips with Tulip Blossom lipstick. I twirl in front of the mirror. I feel glamorous and in control. I feel empowered.

I run my favorite green apple hair serum through my locks and pull them into a side ponytail, leaving my curls kind of loose. When I saw the show in the theatre, that was the way Fantine wore her hair on her deathbed. I will not let my parents affect today. "I can't feel any pain. . . ." I sing into the mirror.

I slide off my shoes and put them in my duffle, so they won't get scuffed in transit. I slide on my flip-flops and grab my car keys from my dresser.

Mom's in the kitchen, her head stuck in the freezer.

"I'm going to my audition." I announce, ready to spin around for effect.

"Good luck." Mom says, as she tosses a box of Hot Pockets on the counter, peering behind the space it occupied for something else.

Tears sting my eyes. She's not even going to look. She's not even going to see who I can be.

I swallow—"Thanks"—and head out the door.

"You look like a movie star." Becca's in the garage digging out her Princess Jasmine scooter. Her jaw hangs open, and she stares at me, like the real Jasmine has just appeared.

"Thanks, Bec." I smile.

"Can I come wherever you're going?"

"Sorry, kiddo." I start toward my car. Her head droops. She cannot come with me. Not an option! But, she looks so sad, and although I'm all about me right now, I don't want to be cruel. "I'll tell you what, when I get home, we can put some of this lipstick and eyeliner on you. What do you think?"

She immediately grins and nods. "Yeah, yeah, yeah! Yippee! Will you do my hair like that too?"

"Sure." I wink. "See ya."

The impossibly heavy metal doors to the auditorium creak

open. It smells like moldy carpet and stale popcorn, but I love that smell—the smell of the stage. The curtains are pulled back, revealing all the things that transform a script into a show: stools—countless stools—ladders, lumber. And there's the old car constructed by the crew that they transform for every show, from Greased Lightning in *Grease* to the family jalopy in *State Fair*. Stairs flank either side of the stage, hidden by a head-high cinderblock wall painted black to make on and off stages easier and less noticeable by the audience. An old baby grand piano on caster wheels sits at the foot of the steps on the left. The seats in the auditorium are hard wood, like the pews at old churches. They squeak when you fold them down to sit. And the room has that always kind of dark feel, like it's always night time—always the night of the performance.

Kate and I make our way toward the first few rows of folding seats.

"I need to hit the restroom," she says.

"Okay."

We're about fifteen minutes early, so I set down my bag and myself in the aisle to stretch. A girl I've never seen before sets her enormous bag down on top of mine. She has long, straight, dark hair, perfectly ironed flat, and large brown eyes framed by spiky mascara-crusted lashes. She's short and curvy and does everything she can to accentuate those curves. She's wearing hot pink fishnets under her black shorts with a matching low-cut, hot pink tank top, with spaghetti straps. The breasts bulging from her skimpy top are bright red.

"I got a little too much sun today," she tells me, chomping a gigantic gob of gum.

"Really? I would have never guessed."

"Yeah, I'm allergic to sunscreen, so I use baby oil, which I know isn't right, but . . ." She pauses to chomp three more times. "I mean, I've grown up with my mom's tanning bed in our basement. I blame her for my sun worship issues."

I smile insincerely. Where did this girl come from? I swear she doesn't go to our school. If she did, I would have noticed her before.

"Have you heard about skin cancer?" I can't help myself. Nobody uses baby oil—that was like what they did in the seventies.

"Yeah, yeah, whatever . . ." This girl doesn't seem fazed. She pushes the pinkest part of her breast with her index finger and watches as it leaves a white fingerprint, then turns back to red. "I'm Natalie. I just moved here from Boston."

"I'm Emma. I've lived here forever." I answer. "How'd you hear about the audition?"

"My drama teacher from my old school sent an e-mail to Ricardo to announce I was coming, and how I'd be perfect for any productions at Spring Hill. Of course, Ricardo sent a message right back inviting me to try out for *Les Mis*. Go figure. I was hoping for something more modern, *Spring Awakening* or *Wicked*, maybe? I'd make a fab Glinda!"

I'm thinking more like Elphaba, a.k.a. the Wicked Witch of the West. Too bad, the rights to *Wicked* haven't been released to the world of high school drama yet. Apparently, no one's clued in Natalie.

The room's starting to fill. Ricardo walks up to the front table dressed in black pants and a blue and orange pinstriped dress shirt. He places a clipboard in front of three seats reserved for the judges and places a pen on top of each clipboard. Next, he takes a longer clipboard and bangs it on the table twice.

Tck, tck, echoes throughout the auditorium.

ANGRY

"Sign in here." He smiles slyly, his moustache lifting to one side. "Name, year, drama classes taken."

"I'm gonna sign in." I nod toward the table and use this chance to escape Miss Tanning Bed.

After filling in my info, I spy Kate returning from the restroom and roam toward her.

"I'm so nervous!" she whisper-screams.

"Me too." I grab her arm. I hadn't been nervous until this very second. I was fine. I was more than fine. I was so excited even to be trying out. But Kate's words hit me in the gut. I wasn't in any shows last year, so all the rest of the drama department has this huge edge over me. "Sign-in sheet's over there." I nod toward the front table.

"Okay, I'm going," Kate says, composing herself.

"I'm gonna sit," I say, plopping down in the aisle seat next to us. I have no interest in dealing with my jitters in the company of the gum-chomping queen.

"Our stuff is up there—" Kate starts, but interrupts herself. "Look, there's Olivia. She supposedly got a voice coach over the summer."

"Great, just what I need—more competition." I bounce my knees too hard. I can tell, because my beaded earrings swing from the motion. I glue my heels to the ground and immediately my dark lilac-painted fingernails start tapping on the arm rests. I roll my eyes at myself.

"Your voice is stunning, Em. Everyone knows it," Kate rasps as she walks to the front.

I look at the clock. Five minutes until show time. My heart beats like the tap shoes of a chorus line. Feet shuffle, seats squeak, and bodies lunge. I feel like I've swallowed one of Ricardo's clipboards. I have got to stand up and move, or I will implode.

"I'm gonna grab our bags," I tell Kate when she gets back.

I try to sneak back to our stuff without having to talk to Natalie again. I'm safe. She's talking to Joshua, who was the male lead in the spring play. He's a great actor, but can't sing on key and trips every time he tries to dance.

"I don't know how I got so short. I mean my mom's five eleven, and my dad's six five, and my two sisters are both tall." Natalie babbles between gum chomps.

"Uh huh," Joshua mumbles, tying his shoes.

"I'm never nervous; I guess I just have a knack for the stage. I get up there, and I *am* the character. I'm just made for the part of Fantine. I mean, I don't look like her, but I can so *be* her," Natalie rambles.

I have my bag in hand and am about to tiptoe back to Kate when Natalie chirps, "What part are you trying out for, Emma?"

I bite my lower lip and turn back toward her. "You don't sign up for certain roles. Everyone just tries out. If you get a part, Ricardo casts you." I fake smile, turn around, and keep walking. She cannot be Fantine!

"This new girl's making me very cranky," I tell Kate when I get back over to her.

"What new girl?"

"The one who thinks she *is* Fantine." I raise my eyebrows.

"Who?"

"I don't know. Her name's Natalie or something. She's from Boston."

"Oh, yeah, I heard about her." Kate sticks out her chest, emulating Natalie's disproportionate bosom. "I think she moved into Adam Galbraith's neighborhood last week and, like, hooked up with him already."

I exhale. I cannot be worried about this girl's love life

when auditions for the show of my life are in—I look at the clock—yikes, one minute. I look upward. Time to get serious.

Hi, God, I know it's been a while, but it's been a rough summer—make that a rough year. But, God this play, I so much want this play. Acting is the best part of me. It's the one thing I'm good at. Please help me get a part. It's all I want. Somehow, I feel if I get to be Fantine in this show, everything else will be okay.

"Ladies and gentlemen . . ." Ricardo's exotic Latin accent echoes off the auditorium walls. All of the shuffling and chattering ceases at his first syllable. He presses Play on his CD player, and the trumpeting of the "Overture" blasts the air.

Goosebumps weave their way through my fishnets. I can barely breathe.

He turns down the music, so it's just eerily playing in the background. "I call off your name, and you come stand on stage. Erin," he motions to the English teacher who always choreographs the musicals, "will teach you a dance step." Ricardo taps his pen on a clipboard.

"Next I will feed you a line, and you will spit it back to me. There will also be singing."

I rub my tongue back and forth over the insides of my bottom teeth like a saw cutting two by fours for the sets.

"Okay? Let us begin!"

The freezing cold heat of anxiety shoots from my stomach to my throat then spreads out toward my lungs, so when I breathe it feels like my chest has been rubbed down with Vicks VapoRub. I press my toes into the ground and lift my heels and gently tap them against the old carpet, up, down, up, down, up, down.

Ricardo's lilting voice lists off name after name. Kate stands on stage, as does Natalie. It looks like everyone who was in last year's musical has found places up there. Is Ricardo putting us in some kind of order? It's not the order of the sign-in sheet, because I was near the top of the list. It's not alphabetical. What's the significance? Where does that put me on his mental list?

Of course, directors should be unbiased and select the cast based on auditions only—except directors are human, and Ricardo knows most of the kids here already. So, he probably already has a short list of students in mind for the leads.

"Emma Monaghan." I'm numb and tingly all over. As if one of the magic strings that make the cast of *Peter Pan* fly is wrapped around my waist, I am pulled to the stage. My bare arm brushes against the curtains as I move toward Ricardo. They are soft and heavy, how I imagine the fur of the Velveteen Rabbit.

"Right here." Ricardo points to one of many white tape Xs on the floor with the toe of his well-polished loafer.

I stand erect, ready. I feel my shoulders roll back and my chin lift. I sneak a glance from side to side without moving my head and am aware of the dramatic black lines rimming my eyes and the powerful pout my blood red lips portray. I am a puppet who's been sitting in her box too long. Now, on stage, I'm ready to come alive. I forgot how exhilarating it is up here, with the lights warming my exposed shoulders and the audience, in this case, judges, cloaked in shadows.

I slide spit around my mouth and swallow to get my wind pipes ready. I press my lips together to even out my lipstick and stretch my mouth.

The dance step is simple. I keep up with everyone else and turn in the right direction and stamp my foot to the beat of the music.

"Now," Ricardo's *w* trills on his tongue, "you will each recite the line, 'Today is my birthday.' I will prompt you with an emotion." He walks slowly and deliberately to the back corner of the stage. Ricardo's a pro at using his large size for effect. He points to Joshua. "Sad!"

Joshua's eyes widen, a little taken aback. I swear it looks like tears fill the corners of his eyes. "Today," Joshua sniffles, "is my birthday."

"Sleepy!" Ricardo points to Cora Hinkle.

"Awwwwy," Cora yawns, "today is my birthday, but I'm too sleepy to care." She stretches her arms to the ceiling then curls up on the floor in a ball. I cringe for her. She broke Ricardo's cardinal rule: don't change the lines. He always says someone went to a lot of trouble to write the lines. That's their job. It's our job to act them out.

My eyes pierce through the crowd, watching each individual perform. There are only so many emotions Ricardo can rattle off, and I don't want to copy anyone else or be outdone.

Ricardo pivots to the front, without finishing the back. "Emma, excited!"

I don't miss a beat. "Today is my birthday!" I exclaim, bending my knees, clutching my hands, and widening my eyes.

After we've celebrated a myriad of birthdays, it's our chance to sing. My vocal chords itch in anticipation.

But instead of getting to belt out one of the beautiful ballads from *Les Mis*, one by one we're supposed to sing, "Happy Birthday to You." I sense a theme. I hope it involves cake at the end. Some people are adding a lot of flair — pretend crying, jumping up and down. If I've got Ricardo pegged right, he wants us to perform things the way they are. There is no drama in this age-old tune, so when it comes to me, I do my best to be precise, to hit each last note.

"That's a wrap!" Ricardo announces. "The names of those selected for callbacks will be posted tomorrow on my page of the school's website. Round two of auditions will be this Wednesday. You all did a wonderful job. Please know if you do not make callbacks, this is not necessarily a reflection of your talent, just perhaps what we were able to see today, or what we require for this particular show." Ricardo bows. "Thank you for coming and have a good evening."

    My shoulders relax for the first time in the two hours that felt like a flash on a camera. I also remember to breathe. I love the clicking sound everyone's shoes make on the hardwood stage as we meander down the wings and back to our gear and our real selves—the selves outside of the performance.

Chapter Ten

I sit straight up at the sound of Billy's chattering from his crib. I've been lying here awake with my eyes closed for a while, wondering when I can check the computer. Billy being awake is the excuse I've been looking for. I creep out of my top bunk and steal a peek at Becca. Her curls peek out from a jumble of covers and baby dolls.

Silently, I pull Billy from his crib to my body and carry him downstairs where I boot up the computer. "Is it morning time?" he asks.

"Yeah, Billy, it's morning."

"Oh good, you're up." Mom's voice interrupts my obsession with the callback list.

"Mama!" Billy squirms out of my arms and runs over to her, which is fine. I click on the internet icon. Our computer is soooo slow. I roll my neck until it cracks. I lick my lips bumpy with sleep slime. I think I forgot to brush before I went to bed last night. Finally! My home page comes up. I type in the school's address and click on Mr. Gomez's name. Nothing!

"Aaahhh!" I scream.

"What is it?" Mom calls. I kind of forgot she was here.

"Nothing," I mumble and shuffle to the kitchen where Mom's getting a granola bar for Billy.

Mom sets him down and hands him the bar. "Emma, your dad said he'd come by today to get the rest of his things." She looks down to Billy as if she's checking on him, but my guess is she's avoiding my eyes.

"And?" I ask. Why is everyone acting like it's totally normal for Dad to be stopping by our house? He's supposed to live here!

"And, I just wanted you to be prepared." Mom ignores my comment and slides her purse on her shoulder. "He said you seemed taken off guard the other day."

Each word she says grates on my flesh. How can she act this idiotic?

"Taken off guard?! For crying out loud Mom! It is not normal! It is not normal for Dad to stop by the house like a neighbor asking for a cup of flour! It is not normal for you to scurry off to work every morning like nothing's changed! It is not normal for none of us to be talking about this! It is not normal for you to be getting a divorce! Normal people do not get divorced!" If I were Wile E. Coyote, red smoke would be pouring out of my ears.

"Oh, Emma." Mom shakes her head. When she blinks, a tear falls. "It's so stupid, but it is normal. One in two marriages ends in divorce. I should have known. Your dad and I were never meant to make it." She snorts and snot actually comes out of her nose, which is completely disgusting.

"So we just keep calling that man who used to live here 'your dad' and go on like nothing happened?" I turn away.

Swoosh. I hear her pull a Kleenex out of the box—thank goodness. "No, but someone still needs to run the store, and Billy still gets hungry, and Dad still needs his freakin' suits for work! So he's coming to get them!" The fire in her voice simmers near mine. "Now, I'm going to the shop, to make a living, to hold this family together. Do you mind doing your part today?" The

ANGRY

heels of Mom's sandals click against our kitchen tile, but I refuse to look at her. I won't give her the satisfaction when this is all so clearly her fault. Well, hers and Dad's, but not mine!

When I hear the garage door shut behind her, I bang my fist on the counter and finally turn around. I will not be here when Dad comes home. I feel like something big and bony and dead has thudded to my stomach, like Hamlet's skull. I hate him! I hate her!

"I am so stupid!" I scream out loud. Why didn't I ask Mom what time he'd be here? I refuse to call her. She'd totally have the upper hand, which is not going to happen. I can take the kids to the pool, but I need to practice today, just in case. I need to sing and act, and I want to watch my *Les Mis Dream Cast* DVD, not to mention I'll be hawking Ricardo's page for the callback list. Okay it is 7:56 a.m. now, and the pool doesn't open until eleven. That leaves three hours. I'll put in the DVD. Billy might like the songs, and I can sing with them, and I just have to pray Dad doesn't stop by until after eleven.

"Hey, Billy." He's still gripping his granola bar with his chubby little fingers, like if he squeezes it tightly enough I might stop screaming.

"Help me with dis!" he demands.

"Sure, bud." I plop down criss-cross-applesauce on the tile floor and peel back the shiny wrapper. "Do you want to watch a movie with lots of crazy people singing?"

"Watch it with me, Em-Em?" he asks.

"Yeah, I'll watch it with you, bud. We'll even sing the songs."

The thick carpet in the family room is soft and comforting to my bare feet. I look down at my coral toenails and wiggle them in the shag. I dig through the green plastic crate of DVDs labeled Emma. "Got it!"

Bennett stumbles into the room, wearing an old, oversized T-shirt with his blanket bunched in his left hand. "Mornin', Ben," I say. "We're watching a movie."

He's not much of a talker in the morning. I can relate. He plops onto one of the white couches and snuggles into its corner.

I punch on the TV and set up the movie. The blast of the "Overture" fills the room. It shoots through my veins and the hairs on my arms stand on end. My feet walk to the beat of the music into the kitchen, which sits right behind the family room. The only thing that separates the two rooms is the island, so I can hear and see perfectly. I pour Cocoa Puffs into bowls and apple juice into cups, all in time to the music. I add milk to mine and Bennett's bowls and grab some spoons, which I drum on the counter on a particularly powerful "Bum bum bum, bum bum bum!" I carry Billy's bowl over to him without milk. He'd just spill.

"Let's eat breakfast while we watch," I tell him. "Bennett, yours is on the counter."

Somewhere before "I Dreamed a Dream," the twins come down, and Billy abandons his food for some trains to zoom. I love this song! I mean this song fills me. I know this is what Ricardo will have us sing tomorrow. *God, please let me be at callbacks tomorrow!*

Callbacks tomorrow! If I make it, I'll have to prepare a soliloquy. I sit upright, throwing my shoulders back. "Perfect posture makes perfect projection." The voice of Mrs. Drake, our grade-school music teacher, rings in my memory. I open my mouth, and Fantine's desperate life comes out of my soul. I belt out the lyrics as if I were the fated Fantine left with nothing. My face is warm and wet. I cannot identify the tears, nor do I want to. I don't know if they are for the beauty of the song or the sorrow of the character or for my own loss and distress of my family—abandoned by my father, fighting with my mother, forced to baby-sit every day, and left with what?

The door leading from the garage opens, and somewhere in the back of my head I hear it, but I'm too lost in the world of a French peasant girl to let it register.

"Daddy!" Anna—or is it Hannah?—screams.

The lights dim, the music fades, the song is over, and so is my reverie. I wipe my wet cheeks with the back of my hand, hoping no one will notice.

"Hey guys!" Dad cheers. "What'cha watching?"

"Who knows?" Hannah answers. "Some weird thing Emma put on."

"You giving a history lesson, Em?" Dad laughs and pats me on the back. I don't have a bra on and feel a bit self-conscious when he touches the T-shirt I slept in.

"*Les Mis*," I say coldly.

"Remember when we saw that in Chicago?" Dad asks like he's here to reminisce about old times instead of taking his clothes to the "new times" he's invented.

"Yeah," I muffle, literally biting my tongue. Of course I remember. It was for my tenth birthday! We went to Chicago to visit my cousins, and the twins were little, and Bennett was a baby, and Becca and Billy didn't even exist. Mom and Dad left the little kids with my aunt and uncle, and we had this special grown-up night out together—just me and my parents. We never got to do that, not since the twins were born. I wore this new purple dress—that was when I was still into dresses—and we took the train downtown. I felt like Cinderella in her ball gown riding in her carriage. I remember being in awe of how tall the skyscrapers were and how the theatre looked like a palace. It had red velvet seats and enormous crystal chandeliers. Gold was everywhere—on the walls, on the ceiling, and lining the prestigious box seats by the stage. I remember asking if it was real gold. I don't remember Mom and Dad's answer. It didn't matter. To me it was real. I swear it was that night when I decided to be an actress.

"Dada, play trains with me!" Billy calls. I allow my eyes to follow him as he runs to Dad and grabs his pant leg.

"Not now, Bill." He cringes, rubs Billy's head, and takes a step back. I can tell Dad doesn't want anything smeared on his suit. "I have to run upstairs and grab a couple of things."

Dad's dress shoes echo on the hall tile and thud up the stairs. I would prefer throwing up to the feeling in my stomach. I return my gaze to the TV. Fire burns inside me. My jaw clenches, and my shoulders square. I pound my hands into the floor, but the carpet is too squishy to give me the satisfaction of a sound.

Chapter Eleven

Billy and I are in the backyard when I hear Dad's truck pull out of the driveway. I'm not sure how long he stayed. I couldn't breathe inside—couldn't physically breathe, like someone stole all of the air in the family room and locked it up in a shoebox and hid it in the back of Dad's closet. All at once the carpet smelled, the movie was too loud, Becca was sucking her thumb, and everyone's bowls were scattered everywhere. I wanted to scream.

I scooped up Billy, ran outside, and plopped him on the swing.

Now, as I push him again and again, back and forth, back and forth, my mind drifts. Soon I'm praying, or talking to God, whatever you want to call it. I'm too out of practice to name it properly.

God, why are You letting this happen? How can Dad be cheating on Mom? How creepy is that? I know they fought a lot, but really, can't You stop this from happening?! Stop this from happening! I shout at God in my mind, demanding Him to rewrite the script of my parents' marriage. *I can't do this! I have enough to worry about. I have auditions looming over me. Please let me make the show, God! Please! Last year sucked! I didn't get to try out for anything because my stupid parents kept grounding me. And the whole thing with Peter and skipping my period made me want to jump off a ledge.*

Billy closes his eyes. "Hiwer! Hiwer!" I give him an overzealous push, and he chortles with glee.

I need a new start. I need a do-over, and a part in this show could be it. I could be beautiful and sing and transform myself into the noble Fantine who gave herself for her daughter. Mom and Dad would be so proud. They would love me again. They'd come and watch together. They'd see Cosette and Marius fall in love, and they'd fall back in love. Peter would come to the show and be wowed by my voice, and he would beg me to be his girlfriend. I might even lose a couple of pounds dancing and prancing around rehearsals every night. Please, God, please! This show means everything!

"Emma," Hannah calls from the sliding glass door.

I turn my head to her and realize my face is, once again, doused with tears. Maybe she won't see from across the yard.

"Phone!" She holds out my cell. I turn back to face Billy, wipe my face as discretely as possible, and wander toward the door.

"Thanks," I tell Hannah, grabbing my phone.

"Hello?" It's too bright out here to read the screen.

"OMG, Em! Congratulations!" Kate's deep voice screams in my ear.

My body temperature drops thirty degrees. My heart pounds like a drumroll. Is it callbacks? Is that why she's congratulating me? I don't dare assume. I've got to know.

"On what?" I ask without breathing.

"Haven't you looked? Ricardo posted callbacks, and your name is on the list!"

"No way!" I inhale.

"Way! Anyway, I wanted to be the first to congratulate you." I hear her catch a giggle on her tongue. "And to ask if I could hitch a ride?"

"Sure." I mumble my mind racing with dance steps and

ANGRY

musical notes and spotlights. "What time?"

"Same as yesterday." Kate's voice is all bouncy.

There's a reason she needs a ride, and she's jumping through the phone. "So, congrats are in order for you too!" I laugh.

"Bingo! Let's go early so we can stretch."

"Deal. I'll figure things out around here and text you back with an exact pickup time, K?"

"K. Later."

I touch "end call." Billy's screaming to get out of the baby swing.

"Sorry, Bill." I tug him upward, but his foot gets stuck, which makes him scream more. Nothing fazes me right now.

I loose him from his plastic prison and swing him around the yard holding tight to his tiny hands. "Em-Em made callbacks, Billy. It's like an answer to a prayer."

Like an answer . . . a smooth voice ricochets in my head.

I was praying, wasn't I? "Yeah, Billy boy, it *is* an answer to a prayer!"

Chapter Twelve

My life is always bit off-kilter. My favorite jeans almost fit, but don't quite button. When I pull my favorite pencil from my backpack, the point is broken. If I reach in the box of Pop-Tarts, all that's left is an empty foil wrapper. But, today, life clicks like clockwork. I told Mom about callbacks, and she seemed vaguely happy for me—happy enough that she agreed to come home early from the The Magic Paintbrush so I could get to school in time.

My fishnets slide on without runs. My makeup goes on without smudging, and there is one last Mountain Dew icy cold on the top shelf of the fridge with my name on it.

I start my car and realize it's full of gas. Yes, it was me who filled it up yesterday, but it's still such a buzz when the planets are in sync. It's like this callback was meant to be.

Think about that for a minute.

This crazy voice inside my head is like Jiminy Cricket in *Pinocchio*, always stating the obvious.

I turn on my radio and bop around in my driver's seat, thinking, just as I was prompted to do. *Okay, God, I'll admit, things are going well, like You've orchestrated the whole thing.* I make a left turn and slow down to avoid tailgating the yellow VW in front of me. *But, God, please let me get this part! Thank You for the callbacks thing. I don't think I've said thank You yet. And it may be*

Your doing, or it may be mine, but I'm over-the-top excited. I really think I can do this. I mean my voice is good and strong, and there's not too much dancing, and I know this show. This could be the thing that changes everything for me. So, please? I guess, I'm begging You again, please?

You're welcome.

I want a "Yes, you'll get a part." Or, "It was all your talent that got to callbacks." Or, "You'll rock today." Instead I get, "You're welcome." *For what? Oh, I get it, because I thanked You. Well, at least You're polite.* Not surprising, God's polite.

I feel a bit humbled. *Can You help me do my best?*

Of course. I thought you'd never ask. I don't remember Jiminy Cricket being such a wisecrack.

Kate's waiting on her doorstep, lime-green messenger bag strapped across her black leotard.

The doors of the auditorium creak as we enter. Natalie turns from where she's huddled with Ricardo to look at us. I feel invisible needles poking the sides of my nose and the joints of my jaw. I hate her! I know I shouldn't. I mean, I barely know her, but who is she, the new girl, showing up in fuchsia fishnets and an aqua leotard that her boobs are hanging out of, palling around with Ricardo like they've been doing shows together for years? Of course, she'll get a part. How can he ignore that body brushing against him?

They go back to their huddle. I hear Natalie's New England accent droning, but I can't make out the words. I look at Kate.

She shrugs and shakes her ringlets. "What are ya gonna do?"

"I'm thinking about bombing her house," I mutter.

"Slightly extreme, but certainly an option." Kate laughs.

Time stands still as if someone's pushed Pause on the remote control of my life, and at the same time flashes like someone's pushed fast-forward. So, after waiting nine hours and at the same time one split second, the first few rows fill with familiar faces of fellow thespians. Ricardo takes his place in front and waves his clipboard around.

"Congratulations for making it to the callbacks. This accomplishment says you have, what they call, a knack for the theatre. Unfortunately, I cannot give parts to everyone who is here today. So," he waves his arm across us, his audience, "if you are not cast for *Les Mis*, I urge you to try out for our winter performance." He glances to his wife, who stands and walks over to the piano.

"Today we as a group will work on the dance. Then, I will have you read the monologue you've prepared, and last you will sing, one at a time, for the solos. When you are done with the singing, you are free to leave. I will post the final cast list on the school website tomorrow."

While his wife's fingers float across the piano keys filling the auditorium with lively, staccato notes, we tap and turn and click through the fairly elementary dance steps. Ricardo positions us male and female, then tall and short, and then mixes us all around, making it impossible to tell who he's watching. The stage lights warm my skin like the sun at the pool. Sweat drips off our swirling bodies, and the smell of body heat and cologne and powder and shoe polish — the perfume of a performance — weighs heavy in the air.

"Take five!" he announces, scribbling madly on his clipboard with his silver Mont Blanc pen.

I guzzle water from my bottle so greedily, it trickles down my chin. I wipe it sloppily with my hand and then chug some more.

Kate laughs. "Need a napkin?"

"Thanks, I'm all right." I snort.

Ricardo appears back on stage, elegant in his lavender dress shirt and black slacks. "Females will sing 'I Dreamed a Dream,' Fantine's solo, and gentlemen will sing 'Who Am I?' Jean's solo. We will do the ladies first. It goes like this."

Mrs. Gomez plays the notes, and Ricardo sings the opening of Fantine's narration of her tragic life. His rich voice is too low for the part, but conveys the tune perfectly, just in case someone was unfamiliar with it. He finishes, looks at his clipboard, and calls out, "Natalie Levine."

I put down my water bottle and watch her strut up on stage. "You will take it up two octaves, Natalie. Ready, set, and . . ." Ricardo points to his wife, and she begins the song again.

Natalie's voice rings out of her short, curvy body, like a bird released from a cage. It escapes her throat and dances with the notes on the piano. All of her nasal, braggadocios tones disappear, and out comes perfection. She doesn't miss a single note.

I exhale when she is done and realize I didn't breathe while she sang.

"Wow," Kate whispers.

"Yeah, wow. I hate her even more. Where did she buy a voice like that?!"

Thankfully Ricardo calls on Ashley, who goes to youth group at my church sometimes. I really like her, but she doesn't project on stage. The audience will never hear her. Next is Kate who does a solid job, but she lacks something. Emotion? Passion? I don't know. She hit all her notes, but her performance seemed flat. I'd never tell her that, though. Next goes Cora. Her voice is pretty, but more of a Cosette than a Fantine. It's a little high for the song, and she doesn't seem to know how to compensate for it. Then Olivia takes her place in the middle of the stage. Her stick straight, long, blonde hair is pulled in a low ponytail. Okay, so her voice lessons really paid off. She hits every note and projects the song all the way out into the parking lot. I feel nauseous. How can I compete with that?

Some other girls take their turns in the spotlight. All have varying degrees of talent, but Natalie and Olivia are standouts. Thankfully enough time and voices pass between them and me that I start to breathe regularly again. By the time Ricardo calls me, I've figured out exactly how I want to deliver this piece. Some girls are on their knees, some add trills to the high notes, but I remember what Ricardo's told me again and again in class. "Perform as it is written." Right now, he just wants me to sing.

"Emma Monaghan." He points to me.

God, please help me do my best.

Give it your all.

There are spiders spinning webs, like Charlotte in *Charlotte's Web*, in my stomach as I walk across the stage to the single microphone placed in the center. My heels clack against the hard wood, echoing through the auditorium as if Ricardo and I are the only people here. I see Kate. She has to wait for me for her ride home. I see Natalie. Figures, she's staying to check out her competition. All the guys watch, too, as they wait for their turns. I feel like the spider webs have taken over my insides and my heart can't beat through them, and my blood can't flow through them, but then I'm standing in front of the mic.

"There was a time . . ." The notes rip through the sticky webbing and stab the air. It is no longer me in front of Ricardo and a bunch of kids I've been riding the school bus with for years. It doesn't matter that my thighs are too big or my parents are freaks or that Natalie can sing like a nightingale and Olivia sounds like she's on Broadway. It is just me and these notes, and the music is me, and I am Fantine. I sing the best I've ever sung. Each note is perfectly placed in the air as if I'm painting a picture on the wall of Fantine's life.

    When I finish I exhale and walk off the stage. I collapse next to Kate and weep. Tears of relief that my audition is over, tears of pure musical joy for such a beautiful song, and tears of disgust for how ugly my real world is. I long to return to the stage and never come down.

Chapter Thirteen

My feet are tied in a knot. I arch and kick and wriggle, but I am confined. I can literally feel my dense hair curling up from the moisture of my sweat. I thrust my legs as hard as I can and roll smack into the white wooden rail of my top bunk.

"Ouch!" I sit up, but only like a mermaid, because I squirmed in bed all night and have tangled myself so thoroughly in my sheets that my legs are like a fishtail of bright orange. I have orange sheets, and Becca has pink. Our walls are sky-blue with hot pink and orange butterfly decals stuck randomly to look like they're flying around our room. Mom calls it a compromise because Becca wanted a princess room and I wanted something more along the lines of PB Teen—you know, brighter and hip. I think the whole thing is a bit third grade and it irritates me even more right now, because those butterflies can flit around, *but I can't move!*

Ummmhhhgg, Becca groans from below. I so don't want to wake her, because once Becca's up, the whole house is up, and I am not ready to deal with all of them today. The thought that's haunted my dreams resurfaces. Is Ricardo's list up yet? This could be the day I turn around my life. He probably decided the cast yesterday at auditions. Even if he had a little arranging to do at home afterward, he certainly knew before he went to bed. Is he an early riser? I have no idea. The two classes I took from him were after lunch period, so I don't know what he's like in the a.m. There's only one way to find out.

I wrestle with the sheets for what feels like half an hour and finally free my feet. I ease my way down the ladder and tiptoe across our floor, trying not to make any squeaks or creaks. I don't hear Billy jabbering yet, so I head down the stairs and sneak into the kitchen.

"Auuhh, auuh." Mom is crumpled at the kitchen table in a short-sleeved brown sweater and paisley peasant skirt. "Ah, hu, hu, hu." Her entire body shakes. Is that a shot glass next to her? I've never even seen her drink.

I feel like I have stage fright—like my feet are glued to the floor, and I physically cannot walk over to her or utter any of my lines, which in this case would read something like, "What's wrong, Mom?"

I don't think I can pull it off. She looks miserable, but this is her fault too, isn't it? She yelled at Dad all the time about being late, about not calling her back, about his evening meetings, and about taking another business trip. The man's a creep, as it turns out, but he works, for crying out loud! Unless . . . unless all those fights were about the affair. About him sneaking off and staying out late. I shake my head. Have I been that stupid? I refuse to think about it. It's too much to process.

I pivot to retreat upstairs. Even Ricardo's list can wait to avoid this emotional disaster.

"Em?" Mom's voice squeaks.

"Hey, Mom. Sorry, I didn't mean to . . . I didn't—I'll just go back upstairs." I don't want her to think I was spying on her. I don't like other people to see me cry.

"No, wait." Her voice cracks.

ANGRY

I stand and look toward her, not knowing what to say. I am perturbed that this is taking over my moment to check the cast list. Mom and Dad aren't the only humans on earth. Why did they have to pick my life to screw up?

Mom reaches out her hand to me. I have no choice but to take it, and she pulls me to the chair next to her. "I'm just soooo," she cries. "So, very very . . ." She can't get out the last word. She doesn't have to. I could fill in a million for her—so sorry for letting you down, so pissed off at your wretched father, so angry at men, so furious with myself. . . .

The pungent smell of alcohol stings my nose.

"Have you been drinking?" This is *not* how I envision families to work. In my fantasy world, Mom would be awake before me with the laptop fired up, all queued up to the school's website. She'd have a Pop-Tart and a Mountain Dew waiting for me, so we could check the list together. Even better, she'd have made pancakes or those cinnamon rolls from a can. Instead, Mom is crippled and leaning on me and drinking—what is it? I scan the counter—Wild Turkey as her crutch. I feel like I will crumple under her weight.

"Just a drop to stop me from shaking. I was trying to unload the dishwasher, and my hands were just shaking and shaking." Mom looks down at her hands. Her left ring finger bears a glaring white tan line where her wedding ring's supposed to be. "I couldn't help it, and it broke, and I can't be breaking people's pottery at the store." I glance at the open dishwasher and the remnants of a cereal bowl shattered into jillions of bits across the floor. She broke a freakin' bowl and just left it there! Mom shakes her head. I watch tears go airborne from her face.

"This is so not fair!" I pound my fists onto the table.

"Tell me about it! Dad wasn't thinking at all! How could he

do this to us?"

She doesn't get it! I mean the whole thing isn't fair! Not just Dad. Her sitting here like a blithering idiot when I need a cheerleader. How can I hold her up, when I can barely stand by myself?

"What's for breakfast?" Becca asks as she pads into the kitchen.

Mom twirls out of her chair and around toward the sink, cowardly hiding her face. She runs the water and grabs a Kleenex.

"Take three giant steps back," I shout in warning, so Becca doesn't cut her bare feet on broken bowl.

"Mother, may I?"

"Yes, you may," I concede.

Becca obeys and looks at me as if I'll continue the game. What the heck. "Twirl around like a ballerina."

"Mother, may I?"

"Yes, you may."

She obliges. I might as well use this to my advantage.

"Hop like a bunny into the laundry room and grab the broom and dustpan."

"Mother, may I?"

"Yes, you may."

Becca bounces off toward the laundry room. I stand from my chair and walk over to the laptop, sitting on the kitchen desk. I punch the silver On button and keep my eyes away from the person formerly known as my mother.

Becca reaches out the broom handle to me. I start sweeping up the slivers of china while Mom stuffs things in her purse. She hasn't even said, "Good morning," to Becca. I want to hit her in the rear with the broomstick.

"Get out six cereal bowls and one box of Cocoa Puffs." I wink at Becca.

"Yeah!" She bounces up and down. I swear the girl could live

ANGRY

off Cocoa Puffs and Capri Suns. "I mean, Mother, may I?"

"Yes, you may."

Mom clears her throat. "I'm off, girls. Have a great day." She managed to get the tears and snot off her face, but her eyes are still red and puffy, and her expression is pinched.

"Bye, Mommy!" Becca hops to the cereal cupboard, too distracted by the game and the sugar to notice.

"Bye. Thanks, Emma." Mom nods toward me.

Right, thanks for saving her hide from looking like a drippy, bippy, drunk cry baby in front of Becca! I smile, but I fear flames will shoot from between my teeth like a dragon.

I dump the ceramic shards of bowl into the trash where they clatter as they tumble into the rest of the rubbish.

The blue screen of the laptop catches my eye. I wiggle the mouse to the Internet connection and type in www.springhillhs.edu.

"Billy's calling for you," Becca announces.

"Okay," I mumble, maneuvering through the site. Old Billy Boy can wait just another minute. *Teachers, Gomez, Cast List.* Okay. It's really up. I didn't know if it would be up this early, but I hoped, and now it is. I can't look. I have to look.

"Emma, Billy's up!" Becca tugs on my nightshirt.

"Yeah, I'll get him in a sec." Goosebumps coat my entire body. Even the inside of my stomach feels prickly and tingly.

Dear God, this is it. Please let my name be here.

I hold my breath and read: Cosette —Natalie

I'm not even going to acknowledge that. I need to keep reading and see what I see.

Fantine —Olivia

Darn! I so much wanted that part. That part was me, but she is a senior, and those voice lessons! Plus, she's so disgustingly tiny and pretty. Pretty girls always get the lead. Okay, I won't let myself freak yet. There's still a chance for something. Did I get anything? My goose bumps have evolved into shivers. I'm as cold as if I've been immersed in snow. Jude — Marius. Boy parts . . . who cares, who cares. . . . Eponine — Emma Monaghan.

My heart stops.

My world stops.

A smile spreads so big across my face that all my teeth show like the Cheshire Cat in *Alice in Wonderland.* I don't move from my frozen spot hunched over the computer, but I cry and shake and laugh. Eponine, the tragic character, the one in love with Marius who's in love with Cosette. Natalie is Cosette. At least she didn't get Fantine.

I scan the chorus, now that I'm breathing again. Inji, Brooklyn, oh, good, Kate got a part. I exhale. She'll be okay with that. I don't think she had her hopes hung on a lead. Getting in is still huge. I would have survived making the chorus. I'd set up in my brain to be excited if I made the chorus. Ashley got in too. Making the show, making *Les Mis,* that's the huge deal. But, I didn't just make the chorus. I got a huge part. *Me!* I actually like this idea of Eponine. I get a gorgeous solo and get to die a tragic death. I actually love Eponine. I am Eponine!

Chapter Fourteen

My stomach feels like the stage curtain being tested—open, close, open, close. I keep feeling jabs under my ribs on both sides.

I pull into Kate's driveway to pick her up for our first rehearsal. She bounces out the door, the curls of her ponytail springing along behind her.

"Hey," she says as she folds her tall frame into my Jetta. "Are we ready for this?"

"You know it!" I shift into reverse. I'm nervous as all get out, but I'm not going to let Kate see that. It's time to click into gear and show everyone what I'm made of. I will prove to Ricardo he made the right choice in casting me.

I turn up the volume and bang my head to the vibration of electric guitars on my stereo.

The auditorium is brightly lit. All the stage and house lights are on. Ricardo sits on stage in a black director's chair, flipping through some papers. Jude and Patrick sit in the front row on the right, laughing—the two male leads, bonding. Kate marches up front and plops her stuff down behind them.

"Hi," Jude says. Jude's a skinny guy. He's about my height, and I'm guessing, weighs less than me. He has shaggy brown hair, kind of like a Beatles mop top and these cool skinny sideburns.

He's a sweater kind of guy. Even though it's summer and he's wearing a red T-shirt and cargo shorts, I picture him in a sweater.

Patrick nods, dark skin glossy from the heat. He wears his hair cut high and tight, like he's in the military, and has a huge smile that overtakes his face.

"Hi, guys." I smile.

"Hi." Kate tilts her head.

I don't think Jude's ever spoken to me before, but that's the cool thing about theatre. We're all in this together now. We're all part of the cast.

Natalie and Brooklyn slide in next to us.

"Ladies," Natalie says, making a big show of swinging her giant, patent leather, designer bag off her shoulder. "Congrats on your parts."

"Thanks," Kate says politely. "You too."

I'm so tempted to ignore Natalie altogether, but technically the girl hasn't done anything unkind. She just drives me crazy!

"You'll make a great Cosette," I force myself to say. I guess I mean it. She *can* sing. The dark hair works too.

"Thanks. You know, I wanted to be Fantine. She's so dramatic, billowing in that white night gown and everything. Think how devastating my cleavage would look popping out the top." Natalie flips her sleek black locks behind one shoulder.

Is she for real?

"But I understand a senior should get that. Plus, I'm new. Everyone would have freaked out if the new girl got that part. Anyway, Cosette gets the guy." She taps Jude on the shoulder. "And you're that lucky guy!" She winks.

Jude turns the color of Natalie's lip gloss. Luckily for all of us, Ricardo stands up and clears his throat.

"Let's give a hand to the cast of *Les Misérables*!" He claps his hands loudly above his head.

We all join in, cheering and stamping our feet like thundering cattle on the auditorium's floor.

"Congratulations to each of you." Ricardo's dark eyes scan the room. "Talent is what got you to this place. Hard work is what will keep you here." His eyes probe mine. Does he wonder if I can hack it?

"Rehearsals will be extremely demanding. Each of you *will* be at every rehearsal, on time, and stay until the end. No exceptions. You *will* give 110 percent of your effort while you are here and also maintain your grades." Ricardo's accent is so rich. His words ebb and flow like violin music. "When we are not rehearsing a part of the performance in which you are directly involved, you are welcome to study, eat, or whatever you like as long as you are quiet and respectful when other actors are on the stage. You *will* be ready when I call upon you." He walks back to his director's chair and picks up a big stack of booklets. "And now for your scripts."

My script simply says *Eponine* on the front. This plain white booklet is more valuable to me than a front-row ticket to a Broadway show. I could marvel at the feel of it in my hands for hours.

After scripts are distributed Ricardo gets us all on stage. "We'll start with music and just basic blocking positions. We'll slowly start adding in dance steps in a week or two, depending on how quickly you master the singing." He calls us up one by one and positions us in what seem like arbitrary spots, but are actually our primary places.

"We shall start with 'At the End of the Day' because it's one of the only numbers where I'll assemble the whole cast. Let's see how we sound together, shall we?" Ricardo claps his hands three times. "You are on the clock now, no?"

We go over the words and the harmonies over and over. I know the lyrics from the soundtrack, but I've never learned the different parts. I try to hit the notes and put the right emphasis as Ricardo directs.

"You are a disgruntled people. You work hard to earn little. You feel overworked and undervalued. You are scraping to get by. And if you do belong to the upper class, you pay too many taxes, and your workers are grumpy. You are outraged with the state of your business, country, and life. Your homeland is in anguish. Your life is hard, and you each have a story to tell. There is to be a lot of anger here, people!" Ricardo's voice crescendos.

I feel like Ricardo is preaching to me. My home is in anguish. My life is hard. I have plenty of anger, and I do have a story to tell. Although, while I am here none of that matters. On the stage I'm not responsible for anyone but me. At rehearsal my dad can't creep me out, and my mom can't make me feel queasy. I don't have to worry about what to say to them or how to act around them or be afraid of what will happen next. Here, in the auditorium, none of that bad stuff can get me. Here, I crave the challenge, the work, and the tingle, like a line of gold light shooting through my body when I hit a note.

Kind of like when you're with Me.

God, I'm assuming that's You talking?

The warm silence that fills me seems to be the obvious answer.

I can't really think about taking time to pray and all that right now. It's way too complicated. Dad is a jerk, and Mom is unstable. I don't know how to help myself, let alone my brothers and sisters, and really if I could just immerse myself in this show and not worry about anything else, that would be perfect.

I look up for Kate or anyone I know to get a break from the

voice inside my head. Jude walks past.

"So, how do you feel about being the rich, educated gentleman around all us peasants?" I ask referring to his role as Marius.

"Like I should buy you all a pizza or something to keep you from starving." Jude smiles. "But since I'm not actually Mr. Have the World at My Feet Marius, I'm just glad I don't have to dress like him every day. I mean tights look great on you, but . . ." He looks down at my legs, and I become completely self-conscious. Then he turns his gaze toward his own thin, muscular, hairy legs peeking out of his running shorts. ". . . they're just not a good option for me."

I laugh. He's pretty funny, which I didn't know if he would be, because he seems so talented and stuff. I like funny.

Chapter Fifteen

I crank up the mix on my docking station while I line my eyes with this shocking vibrant purple color that makes my eyes look ultra green. I grab one of my favorite pairs of earrings, giant, silver circles with turquoise inlays. I love the way they swing when I move my head, plus they're perfect for the aqua and black print top I'm wearing to Noah's party. I'm also wearing jeans even though it's sweltering outside. It gets chilly ice skating. I grab a black hoodie to pop on over my tank when I'm on the ice.

I spritz on a heavy dose of Fendi, and slide on my favorite flip-flops, while singing along with U2. I stuff socks in my purse because I'll need them to skate, and then move a section of curls from one side of my head to the other, creating a side part—better, sultrier. It's been way too long since I've gone out!

I have my keys and my purse and no siblings or pool bags or diaper bags to tote around. I am free!

"Bye!" I call as I head toward the garage. Everyone must be busy. Quite frankly, I don't care who sees me go. I baby-sat all week, and this is my working girl's reward.

"Hey, Em," Mom's voice drones from the laundry room.

I push my tongue hard against my teeth, stopping myself from snapping something obnoxious. I literally feel my shoulders tense in anticipation of the "one more thing" she's going to ask me to do before I go.

"Have you seen Billy's sippy cup?"

I shake my head and stop myself from stating the obvious, "I'm off the clock, remember?" It could lead to Mom changing her mind about my going out, and I will not risk it, not even to speak my mind. Instead I muster every ounce of self-control to say in my sweetest voice, "I think it's on the bookshelf in his room." I throw the words out faster than the heels of character shoes hitting the ground and make a beeline to the garage.

"Thanks. Be home by midnight," Mom calls to my back.

"Right!" I hold my hand with the keys in it high in a wave, but don't look back. This is my night. Everyone else might be celebrating Noah's birthday, but I'm celebrating Eponine and my chance to shine on stage.

I turn on the engine and blast the tunes. I pick up Lindsey, then Raven, then Melissa, then Gracie in order of where they live, closest to farthest.

"We look so hot with our tans!" Lindsey squeals. "Are you girls ready to party?"

"Yeah!" We all scream back. It's been weird this summer with all of us working. Despite our grand plans to see each other every day, we haven't had a lot of nights out. I'm so pumped up; I'm about to burst from my skin.

The party is great. There must be fifty kids here. I guess if you rent out the ice, you might as well fill it. The tunes rock. The pizza is my favorite: pan pizza from Pizza Hut. And I only fall once. We hang out together all night, except when Melissa's boyfriend, Beau, and Melissa do a moonlight skate, as do Lindsey and Noah. Raven and I take full advantage of the situation to make kissy lips and whistle at them as they slide by on the ice. Gracie shakes her head at us and laughs. She'd totally be out there with her boyfriend, Drew, if he wasn't out of town. But besides those two songs, we hang with the girls.

We're getting ready to go, and Lindsey's saying good-bye and happy birthday to Noah, and everyone's trying to unlace their skates with frozen fingers and trade them out for their shoes, when I feel a hand on my shoulder.

"Hey, Emma." It's Peter.

My heart pounds out of my chest as loudly as the music playing over the loudspeaker.

"Hey."

"Want a ride home?" So typical Peter. Ignore me all night and want to hook up in the end. He is cute. And he has that slightly-sweaty, kind-of-cologny smell he always has.

"I drove." I shrug while my brain tries to sort out alternative scenarios. Lindsey could drive everyone home in my car, come back to my house, and spend the night, *or* I could take everyone home and meet Peter somewhere later.

"Maybe next time." He winks. "Just hadn't seen you in a while. Thought we could get caught up, ya know?" He walks away. Just like that. I feel a bit of a stab. So much for alternate plans.

"Good for you, Em." Gracie rubs my back. "I bet he'd like to get caught up!"

"Creep," I mutter under my breath, wondering why I'm disappointed the creep didn't try harder.

"I never know how to tie these laces back together." Melissa plops down beside me with her rented skates in her hands.

Good old Melissa, always defusing bombs without even trying.

"Where's Lindsey?" Gracie asks.

"Uh, pretty sure she's lip-locking with the birthday boy!" I raise my eyebrows, amazed at Gracie's naiveté.

"I thought they were cooling things off." Raven comes over after returning her skates.

"Right," I say as sarcastically as possible.

Lindsey and Noah emerge from the locker bay. Lindsey's looking up at him like Juliet does to Romeo in the balcony scene. He leans over and kisses her on the lips. Just quick and sweet, but we all see it.

"She doesn't want a boyfriend, and she gets *that*." Raven pouts. "Why doesn't she save some for her besties who actually want a guy?"

"I miss Drew," Gracie sighs.

"Enough already," I groan. "How about we substitute a caffeine high for the love buzz? Who wants to go to Morning Brew?"

"I'm in," Lindsey dreamily says as she drifts away from Noah and back to us.

"A little chai always does me good," Raven echoes.

"Okay," Melissa says, "I'm stuffed. Coffee is about all I have room for."

There's an awkward pause. Melissa has this eating disorder, and whenever she brings up food we're all a little tongue-tied. I'm relieved when Gracie breaks the silence.

"Maybe a mocha will warm my lonely heart." She fake cries, "Boo-hoo."

"P-leease!" I announce. "Iced lattes await us!"

We cram into my Jetta and head over to Morning Brew.

Melissa opens the door, and the freezing blast of air conditioning hits us in the face, but not as hard as the image of my dad sitting at the first booth with his arm around Carol. Raven and Melissa are already walking toward our usual seats, the barstools at the counter. Gracie and Lindsey are stuck behind me. My pulse zooms to the moon. This was my night, fun with my friends, no worries, for once. And then—*smack*—he has to punch me between the eyes! I rush to Dad's table and growl, "Fancy seeing you here."

"Emma, what a nice surp—"

Fire boils inside me. How can he act cool and composed? This is not a social visit. "Get over yourself!" I shoot imaginary lasers from my eyes. I wish they were real. I wish I could burn him. "You are such a prick!" There isn't a word strong enough for me to call him, but I'll keep on trying. "You are such a—"

Someone grabs my arm and yanks me backward, like a crook pulling a bad performer off stage. In the instant I feel the tug, Dad's steel eyes pierce mine. He glares, then turns back to Carol and laughs, dismissing me altogether. The crook turns me around and pushes me out of the shop. My throat burns where more words want to jump out and attack. Scathing words that want to scratch him and bite him for all the pain he's causing me. Can't he see how much he's hurting me?

"It's okay, Em," Lindsey tries to reassure me. Her face is attached to the arm that pulled me out of there.

"He acted like it was normal!" I yell. "He acted like bumping into him with his mistress was what we do every weekend."

"What was he going to say, Em?" Gracie's voice is calm and even.

"Don't you dare stand up for him!" I shoot Gracie a glare. "I need you to stand up for me!"

Gracie turns and walks back inside, but I yell after her, "He could have said, 'Wow, this is so embarrassing' or 'I'm such an absolute jerk!'" The pressure inside my head pushes tears out in a steady stream. My whole head is preparing to explode. "Or how about, 'I'm so sorry. I never meant for you to see . . .'" My voice shakes and my words are all garbled. I collapse on the curb, lean over, and proceed to puke. I loathe him! How can he do this? How can he sit there so smug and laugh me off while I'm out here barfing?

Gracie returns with Melissa and Raven.

"Let's get out of here," Lindsey whispers.

Gracie hands me a Kleenex from her purse, which of course makes me angry, because I'm supposed to be mad at her, and she's being nice, and I know that deep inside, but I need to be p.o.'d at someone. I wipe my mouth.

Melissa gives me a piece of gum. "It helps a little." She smiles weakly. Miss Scarf and Barf probably speaks from experience.

Lindsey pries my keys out of my clenched fist. "I'll drive."

The car ride is silent, except for my sobs.

"I'm sorry," Raven says and puts her hand on my shoulder.

"It's not your fault," I hiss. "It's his! What an absolute—" Well, I use some words I probably shouldn't use.

"We're here for you." Gracie hands me another Kleenex.

"I thought only moms had Kleenex in their purses." I'm just trying to lighten the mood, and maybe get back at Gracie a little for defending Dad.

She doesn't respond.

Melissa's voice is almost a whisper from the backseat. "You all have been so great to me. I learned I couldn't face my problems alone." She inhales loudly. "If you need us, Em, or if you want someone to pray with." Her voice is swallowed by the silence.

I can't answer her. I don't want to feel better. I don't want people telling me it will be all right. It's too big and too painful to let go. What my dad did is horrific! Unforgivable! I want to shout and stamp and rage!

Lindsey drives around town for a while allowing my sobs to soften into a slow trickle of tears. She takes everyone home, one by one, saving me for last. When Raven is delivered to her doorstep, Lindsey turns to me and says, "You want to spend the night?"

"Yeah, but my mom will flip if I don't come home, and—" I look at the clock on the dash, 11:53 p.m. "It's too late to call."

Lindsey puts the car in reverse.

"Screw it! Sure. There's no way I can go home. I can't. . . ." I swallow the tears wanting to fall. "I just can't," I whisper.

Lindsey turns toward her house. She slides her hot pink phone from her pocket and dials my house. I can hear from where I sit the phone ringing and ringing. Finally there's a click and my mom's voice on the machine.

"Hey, Mrs. Monaghan, this is Lindsey. Emma's had a tough time tonight, with the divorce and all." She looks at me. "So she's sleeping over at my house. She'll drive home in the morning. Thanks."

"Done." Lindsey announces to me as she snaps her phone shut.

I breathe, I think for the first time since I saw him. That creepy look in Dad's eyes was the exact look he gave me that day in the closet when I found *the box*. I shudder and push the image of him out of my brain.

"So, Lindsey," I say, regaining a bit of spunk, "what *is* up with you and Noah?"

Lindsey bangs her head on the steering wheel. "I thought your dad was enough of a diversion for no one to notice."

"So, you told Dad to bring a date to the coffee shop to protect yourself?" I fake accuse.

"You're so on to me." She laughs. "And my plan was working so splendidly."

Chapter Sixteen

"Emma Katherine!" Mom screams when I walk in the front door.

"Hi, Mom. Good to see you." My tongue rubs the smooth evenness of my top teeth where there used to be the bumps of braces.

"Were you too drunk to come home?!" she shouts.

"What?" I ask. Where did this line of questioning come from? My insides are on fire.

"I get a call, around midnight, according to the answering machine, that you and Lindsey planned an impromptu sleepover." She slams her coffee mug on the counter. I notice an open bottle of bourbon next to the coffee pot.

"Who's calling *who* drunk?" I throw back at her.

Mom glances back at the counter. "This, young lady, is about you, not me!"

"Really want to know what happened last night?" I dare her.

"I'm waiting!" she shouts back.

Billy appears from nowhere and climbs into my arms. Out of the corner of my eye, I see Bennett slink up the stairs.

"I was not drinking, unlike some people around here. I went to get a *coffee* and saw Dad all kissy kissy with Carol at Morning Brew!"

Mom's eyes flash with hate and then glaze over with tears. I don't care. I can't believe she tried to turn this on me. It's like she doesn't even consider how this affects me!

"I—I . . . don't know what to do with you!" Mom screams, turns, and heads outside, but not before picking up her spiked coffee.

I'm stuck. There's nowhere for me to run. No stairs for me to climb or door for me to step out to escape. Billy pulls on my shirt. "You happy now, Emma?"

I shake my head. "Poor Bill. It's not your fault either. We'll stick together, okay?" I whisper.

"Mommy not happy," he announces.

"No," I answer. I see a window of opportunity here. "Why don't you go out there and give her a hug. It will make her feel better."

"Okay." Billy be-bops toward the door. I open it for him, and once I see he's climbing onto Mom's chair, I close it behind him. I need to escape. Where can I go to get out?

I grab my iPhone, slide in ear buds, select music from *Les Mis*, and open the front door. I slam it behind me. No one cares where I am anyway. I walk and walk around our neighborhood.

I turn left at the stop sign and walk along the wooden bridge that flanks the duck pond. Frustrated with *Les Mis* for not cheering me up, I touch Shuffle, letting my phone pick the next tune for me. I lean over the rail.

"My hope is in You!" the lead singer from Third Day bellows in his Georgian drawl. My hope is in You? I laugh at the irony.

So, if I hope in You, God, then what?

Then you can let go of all that anger inside.

Oh really, You noticed? I am a bit ticked.

Apparently God isn't amused. I don't hear anything back.

ANGRY

I let the music keep playing and think about it. Why should I hope in God? Well, I have nothing to lose if I hope in Him, but what is it exactly I'm hoping for? For the first time all summer, I wish we had youth group this week. Lindsey and I go during the school year, and although I go mostly to get out of the house and have some face time, I have to admit I usually feel better after I go. I'm not super into God or anything. But, it's nice to know someone out there loves me, and to hear I'm forgiven for all the junk I do (even if I'm not so sure), and for someone to say there is hope for this messed up world. There it is again, that word, *hope*.

I circle back toward the house, not ready to face the world. My phone buzzes midtune. It's a text from Raven.

What time r we going 2 pool? Who's driving?

I completely forgot. We all planned to have a big pool extravaganza today. We're going to stay until it closes—the perfect distraction from my at-home drama.

Chapter Seventeen

"Right. Now, when it is for real, we will have scenery. So, the chair—" Ricardo points to a chair in the wings. "Kate, please fetch that chair." He winks a thanks to her. "It serves as a storefront and that bench"—he indicates the bench in front of the piano—"will be over here." He nods to Patrick who scurries down the steps and returns with the bench.

"Good. Good. Okay, people. We must use our imaginations. These are not things to sit upon; they are part of the Paris street front. And this is not a high school stage; this is an avenue in France. And you are not American teenagers; you are French men and women, husbands, wives, shopkeepers, beggars, students."

Goosebumps prickle my legs.

"The entire cast needs to be on the stage. Today is our day of dancing! We will start with 'At the End of the Day.'" Ricardo waves his arms toward the stage. "Places, everyone!"

There's a shuffling and squeaking as everyone mounts the steps toward our tape Xs. "You will give Erin your full attention." Ricardo nods to our choreographer.

She directs us like puppets, rapidly running over dance steps and expecting us to imitate. "Now, step, slide, step, slide, hands on knees, turn, look right. Other way, step, slide, step, slide, jump on one foot, and front row—you'll scoot back like this. Back row, you'll scoot forward to trade places with the front row. Got it? Let's try! Five, six, seven, eight!"

We scoot and slide and swivel and sweat. We're chanting the lyrics along as we dance, not singing, which can strain our vocal chords, but keeping time with the words, because that's how we know this music. We stomp and scoot and fill the stage and make it come alive.

Mrs. Gomez plays the same notes over and over on the piano. Erin's voice calls out again and again, "Now ones turn, and twos turn, then threes turn, that's right. Everybody spread out! And one more time, back before the turns. Right! And five, six, seven, eight."

Clap, clap, clap!

"Okay, people, that will be enough for today." Ricardo wipes sweat from his brow with his pink, starched sleeve. "Enjoy your weekend and practice, practice, practice."

After two hours of dancing, I'm whipped, and I don't think I could go on, but time has not existed while I've been here. It's just been the stage and the sounds of shoes shuffling against wood. I haven't been annoyed by Natalie or jealous of Olivia for getting to be Fantine or distracted by Jude's cute sideways smile. Well, maybe just a teeny bit distracted. But my parents don't even exist here. I haven't wondered if someone was better than me or if I was better than them. I've just danced.

I exhale for what feels like the first time since I got here. "Wow!"

"Whoa, is more like it for me," Kate says between gulps for air. "I thought I was in good shape from swimming, but I am whipped."

"Yeah, intense, right?" I smile. "That rocked."

"You're crazy." She rolls her eyes at me.

"Maybe." I nod. "Maybe."

Chapter Eighteen

Rrrriiiiippp.

I pull off a large sheet of brown craft paper from the enormous roll and tape it over the edges of the wooden table in the corner where a group of women are having a baby shower tonight. I take a tile Mom has painted "Reserved" in cutesy pink and blue letters and prop it on a stand on the table.

"Thanks, Em," Mom says as I clear a bowl of murky water and soiled paint brushes from another table.

"No problem."

I love my mom's store. I really do. I love the thick, chemical smell of paints and the bright, lime green walls. She plays a great mix of coffeehouse tunes over the speakers, everyone from Matt Nathanson to the Goo Goo Dolls to Jack Johnson. Mostly I love the shelves stacked with dull white pottery, full of possibility and endless outcomes. Any of the picture frames, coffee mugs, or statuettes can be transformed into works of art or tokens of love or permanent fixtures in people's homes. I was actually excited when Mom asked last night if I could work at The Magic Paintbrush this afternoon. One of her workers, Marissa, called in sick, and Dad had been asking for a time to take the little kids to the park, so he's baby-sitting while I fill in Marissa's shift.

Totally weird that Mom used the words *baby-sit* and *Dad* in the same sentence, like she had to hire him to play with his kids. I also don't know if I should feel slighted or relieved that I wasn't in on this "visit." I don't have any idea what I'd say to Dad. I don't know how I feel about him anymore. I mean he's still my dad, I guess. But what a jerk! I can't believe he did this to Mom, to all of us. I'm in high school. These are supposed to be my best years, right? If these are the best, I don't want to see the rest.

I still can't believe Dad stood there that day in his closet and made me feel like a criminal when I found his precious "Carol box." He was the one who had something to hide. Or the night on the porch when he got me out of trouble for coming home late—it was just to cover up the fact that he'd been on the phone with *her*. Has he ever been nice to me for real? Who knows if he hasn't been manipulating us our whole lives to run around with women or whatever it is that gives him a thrill?

"Why does a banker have to go on a business trip?" Lindsey had asked me one time. I'd shrugged and blown it off naively. Now I'm wondering if it was really a business trip.

"Excuse me." A little girl tugs on my apron.

"Yeah." I look down. I wonder how long she's been standing there.

"Do you have more pink?" She holds up an empty bottle of Princess Pink.

"Sure." I smile. Princess Pink is Becca's favorite color too. I head in the back room that smells like crisp paper and cleaning supplies. I locate the pinks and refill the small bottle for the girl with the chocolate eyes and orange shirt.

"Here you go, sweetie." I hand it to her. "What are you painting?"

She looks at me shyly and takes the bottle. "Thank you."

"Do you mind if I look?"

She nods her head three or four times, and I follow her to the table where she's working with her mom and little brother. She's covering a small unicorn with countless coats of pink and sparkly blue.

"It's beautiful." I wink. "I can't wait to see how it fires up."

I go back to the sink and finish rinsing out the dirty brushes and fill the bowl with fresh water.

"Em, do you have a sec?" Mom calls from the counter at the front of the store. It serves as her office with its flat surface, computer, and drawers, as well as the checkout. From this elevated perch she can greet everyone who comes in and keep her eye on the whole shop.

"Sure." I replace the fresh bowl and brushes on the reserved table.

"You know Dad's with everyone else right now."

I nod. The muscles in my stomach stretch like taffy being pulled.

"He wants to see you too."

A small peep escapes my lips. In a way I'm relieved he hasn't completely forgotten about me. In another, I'm horrified to see him.

"You're older. He wants to talk to you one on one. When Anne comes in to work the baby shower, we'll head home, and you can go out to dinner with him." Mom's eyes are on the papers that litter her desk.

"What if I don't want to?" I ask. I hate being backed into a corner.

"Emma, this isn't easy on any of us." Mom takes off her glasses and rubs her eyes. The smile lines around her eyes look like full-fledged wrinkles. She's aged about twenty years in the last couple of weeks.

"I'll help with the baby shower. We could reschedule."

"I think you deserve to ask him some questions and tell him how you're feeling." Mom ignores my suggestion and exhales. "He's taking you to Pizzaro's."

The thought of stromboli loaded with sausage and dripping with cheese is slightly tempting, but I still feel like I've been duped.

The store's pretty slow as it approaches dinnertime. I decide to transform round drawer pulls into soccer balls for Hannah and Anna's upcoming birthday. When there are lulls in refilling paints, cleaning tables, and ringing people out, I paint white backgrounds and black octagons with a tiny brush on eight smooth circles. I can't allow myself to think about dinner. Every time my mind wanders to Dad's face, I feel a strain in my throat, like a piece of Play-Doh being stretched into a snake. I avert my thoughts. How would Eponine handle this? Her dad's a jerk too!

My character would go out to dinner, because she was basically starving and could use the meal. Plus using someone as evil as her dad couldn't be all bad, could it?

Chapter Nineteen

When we pull into the driveway, Mom says, "I'm just going to stay in the garage for a minute. Go on inside. Tell your dad to meet you outside, and tell the kids I'll be inside in just a second." She squeezes my hand too tightly.

The whole way home I've been agonizing about what I'm going to say to Dad, about how much I don't want to see him. Then this, "Your dad," from Mom! How awkward is that? Her hand squeeze is so desperate. I'm the one who has to face the guy, while she hides out here with the shovels and folding soccer chairs.

"Sure," I shrug.

On the way to Pizzaro's, Dad chitchats about the Denver Broncos and the monkey bars at the park where he took the kids. He tells me about the new teller they hired at the bank and asks when school starts and if I've been going to the pool much. I answer in one- or two-word answers.

Who does he think he is? He never asked me about any of this stuff before. He thinks he can just sleep around on Mom, move out, and then all of a sudden become one of my pals? He's either relentless or oblivious. He just keeps gabbing as if I were actually engaged in this conversation.

The smell of Pizzaro's melts some of my defenses. Garlic and fresh-baked dough get me every time. We sit in a booth near the back.

After the owner with the grey moustache and round belly brings us water and bread sticks, Dad's tone of voice changes.

"Emma, I know you must be pretty hurt by all of this, but I want you to know none of it is your fault."

"My fault!" I retort, daring him with my eyes to say otherwise. Like I ever thought it was my fault.

I pick up a breadstick and contemplate throwing it at him. Instead I break it open. Steam pours out of the center. My fingers twinge from the heat. I dip it in tangy tomato sauce and let the buttery, garlic flavors dance on my tongue.

"Don't get upset." Dad sits back. "I just want you to know that what's going on is going on between Mom and me, and it doesn't have to affect our relationship at all."

I reach for my water and slug some down too fast, making it shoot up my nose. *What relationship?* I think. I mean really, how would I define my relationship with Dad? He works. He comes home. He eats dinner with us and jokes around for a few minutes each day. He doesn't know my friends or very much about me, really. He doesn't even know I'm in *Les Mis*, which is basically all that matters in my life right now. And, how can he call Mom "Mom"? It sounds too familiar for him to be allowed to use. You know like in some foreign languages there's the "formal" *you* and the "personal" *you*. I think he should switch to the formal version.

I come back with, "What you've done affects everybody!"

Dad strokes his chin as if he's processing my statement.

"Can I take your order?" Brock Bulthaup, Lindsey's date to the Sugarplum Stomp freshman year who has sprouted a bad case of acne but has a great sense of humor, stands by our table with a notepad and pen. Just what I need—kids from school knowing my dad's running around on my mom.

I roll my eyes toward Brock, signaling I'm embarrassed to be here with my dad.

"Two sausage strombolis, extra cheese." Dad winks at me, confirming this is the perfect order.

It is the perfect order. I wish I had the guts to contradict him and pick a salad or something. But there's no way I can resist the stromboli, and he knows it.

The food is outrageously delicious. I stuff myself with cheese, dough, sausage, and garlic until my stomach feels like it's going to bust.

"You know, pumpkin"—he totally tries to lure me in with the nickname he gave me when I was born because of my orange hair—"things with Mom and me have been rocky for a long time. One day I was working at the bank, and Carol came in to get a loan." He looks me directly in the eye and talks in that hypnotic voice of his. "She was so attentive and interested in my work. I mean, when was the last time anyone at home asked about my job?"

I consider that. I never asked about his work. Quite frankly, banking bores the socks off me. I can't remember Mom asking him about his job either, although she always goes on and on about The Magic Paintbrush. I never thought about it, because I didn't care. I look at Dad. He's noshing on stromboli. He looks peaceful and happy. Did that really bother him, and is he happy now? Or did it never really bother him at all? He doesn't look bothered. Were his feelings hurt? Did he feel like I do about *Les Mis*—like no one at home cares? Or is he just using these lines to sway me? I can't stand to be manipulated!

Dad swallows some water. "Carol came in a handful of times to complete her paperwork, and we got to know one another. She loved her kids. She loved coaching. Just like me." He gives a weak smile and shrugs his shoulders, as if to say, "Can you blame me, Em?"

"You know, some days I wonder if your mom loves our family as much as she loves The Magic Paintbrush." He shrugs again and cuts into his food.

I wonder that sometimes. I press my tongue against the insides of my teeth. This is so not fair. We came here to talk about him. I wanted to blame *him* for everything *he's* done, and now I'm wondering about *Mom*. All of a sudden I want to slap her for not asking about interest rates and for being obsessed with new paint colors.

Dad reaches across the table and holds my hand. As if he can read my mind, he says, "I know, honey. I've been feeling neglected by her for years. I just wanted you to see where I was coming from, and I can tell you do." He nods knowingly.

He understands. What? He understands nothing! What an absolute weasel. He and Mom may have problems, but he's trying to turn me against Mom. She's the one who talked me into coming tonight. If it weren't for her, I wouldn't even be speaking to him. I was almost taken in by his hypnotism.

"Nice try, Dad. Ever heard of counseling? Talking it out? Mom doesn't sit around jawing off about you, and by the way, you're the one who cheated on her!"

"I know you're angry and confused," Dad calmly responds. "This is a lot for someone so young to have to go through. I just want you to know what happened has nothing to do with you, and I want us to still be friends."

"I have friends." Friends? When were my dad and I ever friends? Who wants to be friends with their dad? And young? Does he think I'm twelve?

ANGRY

I'm so over him and his wordsmithing. I push my plate away.

We're almost home when Dad puts out, "Emma, I'd like to do this again soon. I'd really like to spend time with you and keep up with what's going on with you."

I uncontrollably snort out of my nostrils. Is he that clueless, or does he think we had a good time?

"Maybe next time Carol could come with us. I'd love for you to get to know her. You'd love her, Em."

We pull into the driveway.

"Shut up!" I shout at him. My skin prickles like when I get sunburned. There is so much wrong with his suggestion, I don't know where to begin. "If you'd wanted me to get to know her, you could have asked me to join you at Morning Brew!"

I get out of his car and slam the door as hard as I can. I will it to shatter into a million pieces, but my magic powers haven't been working very well lately. Seeing it still intact, I punch the glass as hard as I can. I imagine the window cracking into a zillion shards, but the only thing damaged is my fist, which stings, and my pride. Tears gush down my face. I run inside and straight to my room where I slide on pj pants and a T-shirt and crawl into my bed.

I curl under my covers like I'm five again. Sobs rack my body. I try to muffle my mouth in my pillow, so no one will hear. I cradle my sore knuckles with my left hand. Hot tears flood my face. I grab my teddy bear, Brownie, and hold him tight against my heart, hoping he'll keep it from hurting so much.

God? What am I supposed to do? I hate him! I hate him! What does he think he's doing—pretending we're old bowling partners? Why does he think he can just waltz into my life and start a relationship we never even had? It's all so phony! You say we're supposed to love everyone. Does that include him? Does that include Carol, who

I may hate even more than Dad? What if he marries her? Then I'd have to talk to her, because she'd be my stepmom. And all that stuff he said about Mom. Is any of it true? Did she ignore him? Did she put the store before their marriage? Does that justify what he did? I am so angry! Lord, help me not be so angry! I want to break something or hit my dad square in the nose or cut Carol's pretty blond hair with pinking shears. Jesus, You were so kind to people who were mean to You—like those soldiers who nailed Your hands. You said You forgave them. How did You do that? I don't even want to do that!

I feel like Eponine crumpled on the pavement after she's been shot, only there is no strong Marius to hold me in his arms.

Chapter Twenty

We've officially moved from the school stage to rehearse at the community college, where the performances will take place. It's foreshadowing that summer's almost over, and we only have three days until the start of school. Entering the auditorium of the community college from the ninety-four-degree parking lot is like entering a secret world. The heat and brightness of summer disappear in the darkened room where only the stage lights illuminate.

The smells of mowed grass and blacktop melt away to antique velvet curtains and the squeaking of fold-down chairs. Outside there are no walls to hold anything in. It seems my emotions this summer have been flying every which way, but in here, in this special place carved out of the rest of the world, all that matters is the show.

I feel like Frank Sinatra when he sings "New York, New York," "If I can make it here . . ." I've arrived. I made it. I'm empowered. I feel at home here, even though I've never been inside this building before. This isn't just singing in the shower, or reading a skit in acting class. This is real.

The cast and crew have become really close—going through all these intense rehearsals together, seeing each other day in and day out. I could go sit with anyone and strike up a conversation, but I don't want to right now. I want this moment to myself.

I find a seat at the end of an aisle on the left and set down my bag. I slide on my character shoes and breathe in the auditorium.

There's a buzz in the air. A couple of guys from the chorus laugh in the row in front of me and slap each other's backs. Gym bags, purses, and backpacks plop on the floor and thespians plop into seats.

Natalie's voice booms throughout the auditorium, "Of course we took a little trip to do all of my back-to-school shopping at Nordstrom's. Their salespeople are the only ones who are really helpful at finding clothes that fit. It's so hard for me to find clothes to fit me because I am thin and short and have all the right curves, you know?" I see her now, flipping her hair. "At least I'm not chubby like some of our leads." I want to slap her, but I won't let her ruin this moment for me. This is my moment to savor.

Jude — or should I say "Marius"? — joins the group of guys in the row in front of me. He glances toward me, smiles, and raises his eyebrows. Wow! I'm so busted staring at him. I smile a quick smile and look down to my shoe buckle, as if I hadn't already adjusted it. He's way cooler than Peter. What was I thinking with Peter? I'm not saying Jude would ever like me or even that I like him, but he's this guy with a real talent, and he loves theatre, like me, so we actually have something in common. Peter was so about something else; I'm just not sure what that something was.

Ricardo appears on the stage and bellows in his rich, lilting voice, "Ladies and gentlemen, you are *Les Misérables*!"

His voice sinks into my skin which begins to tingle.

"Curtains."

Somewhere from backstage, a crew member opens the heavy, red velvet curtains to reveal the magnificent sets. Towers and gateways and ramps connect an elaborate depiction of nineteenth-century France. In the middle of it all is a turntable thirty feet in diameter—the infamous rotating stage that makes the sets of *Les Mis* literally come alive. Dancing and walking on the turntable will be completely different than the stationary stage we've been rehearsing on at school.

"This is the most difficult show I've ever directed. *Les Mis* is a masterpiece, but it doesn't pull itself off, no? It takes an exorbitant amount of work, as is shown by the work of our crew." Ricardo waves his arms toward where the crew is huddled on the steps. "Let's give them a hand, shall we?"

We all clap and stomp and hoot, and then Jude and Patrick stand up, starting a standing ovation. I stand too. Very cool! The crew totally deserves a standing O. The set is like a fairy tale.

"Bravo." Ricardo's voice booms above our cheers. "Now, let us get going!"

Patrick sticks his fingers in his mouth and blows a loud whistle. I feel energy jumping out of me, pulling me out of my seat.

The orchestra is here today, sitting in chairs hidden below the stage in a small pit. They play the music they've been practicing on their own, while we've been practicing the words. I've loved listening to Ricardo's wife play the score on the piano, but as soon as I hear the horns and strings, her music seems flat and empty in comparison. The orchestra's music seems as alive as the moving stage, as our own bodies versus the printed script. This is no longer a play to me, but a living, breathing thing.

"We will work on each of the large numbers today to try to get a feel for our magnificent sets. First, as always, 'At the End of the Day'!"

After the song, I collapse in my seat and chug some water, while breathing in the enormity of performing in a place like this. Kate and most of the other girls assemble on stage for another big number, "Lovely Ladies." I'm not on, so I can chill for a bit. I pull out my phone to text Lindsey. But Ricardo's voice, rolling like gentle thunder before a storm, stops me in my tracks.

"Stop the music, please!" Ricardo walks to the edge of the stage. "What is the trouble, Miss Olivia?"

Olivia, the girl who plays Fantine, slumps near the side of the stage, tears streaming down her face.

"My voice," she squawks. "I can't s-s-sing." Her entire body shakes and she looks down at her feet.

Inji, her best friend, rushes to her side and puts her arm around Olivia, as if Inji's literally holding up Olivia, so she doesn't crumple.

"What do you mean," Ricardo's voice crescendos, "your voice?"

Olivia takes deep breaths.

I'm frozen in my seat. What *does* she mean?

"It was hurting a little last week," she rasps, "but I didn't think anything about it." Olivia wipes her eyes with her bone of an arm, smearing her powder blue eyeliner across her cheek. "I took it easy this weekend, sucked on a lot of throat lozenges, practiced dancing, but didn't really sing. You know, to give it a break." Olivia's voice has dwindled to a whisper, but there's no problem hearing her. The entire cast and crew are hanging on her every word.

"And now?" Ricardo stands directly next to her. I didn't even see him mount the stage, but there he is.

Olivia shakes her head and starts crying again.

"And now, my dear, you must rest." Ricardo takes Olivia's arm from Inji and guides her down the steps. "You will attend rehearsals, but sit on the sidelines for the rest of the week. You will also . . ." Ricardo grabs his legal pad and pen and starts scribbling. We all watch as intensely as if it's *The Mystery of Edwin Drood* and the murderer is about to be revealed. "Drink this."

ANGRY

Is this really happening? Did Olivia really just lose her voice and get dismissed from singing for an entire week? If she does get better, which is still an *if* here, will she be ready in time for the show with a whole week of downtime?

"This is a recipe for tea." Ricardo hands her the paper.

Olivia, still sniffling, furrows her plucked brows.

"Trust me. It works," Ricardo booms. "And lay off the lozenges. You all hear that?" He looks up at the rest of us. "Lozenges only cause more damage. Lay off the lozenges!" He growls like a grizzly bear. Then, "Take five," he calls out over his shoulder indicating we need to give him time to figure things out.

Since I was ten, I've longed to be Fantine. But after all this time singing and dancing around in Eponine's skin, I feel like maybe Eponine is actually my dream role, and I just never knew it before. But now what happens to the role of Fantine? Technically, Brooklyn is her understudy. Can Brooklyn hack the demands of Fantine? Her voice is nasally. Would Ricardo let me take over Olivia's part and have Brooklyn take over mine? Would I want to? I shake my head. I don't think I could let go of Eponine. Part of me has become her. And in a weird way, I feel like part of my character has become me.

There's also that creepy, selfish, deep, dark fear that if Olivia lost her voice, I could lose mine too. My hand strokes my vocal chords while my tongue presses against my teeth — hard.

God, please don't let me lose my voice!

"As you all know, the show must go on!" Ricardo practically roars at us, like it's our fault Olivia has laryngitis. "Brooklyn, you'll take over the role of Fantine, and we'll take 'Lovely Ladies' from the top. Ready, and — " Ricardo points to the orchestra, and they scramble to produce the opening chords.

That settles that.

I exhale. Jude turns back and looks at me nervously, shaking his head, one eyebrow cocked. Clearly this is not the right time to chat, but I'm guessing he's equally concerned about Olivia, his voice, and Brooklyn in the lead.

Ricardo drills us hard to make up for the break, or for Olivia's voice, or maybe for Brooklyn's voice—I don't know—but he is *not* happy. I repeat NOT happy. Over and over we practice the main numbers while the stage spins, squeamish about our footwork, falling down and picking ourselves up again. Over and over, the conductor restarts the orchestra, until the timing of our voices finally melds with the timing of their chords.

"I tire of people tripping on the stage." Ricardo seems exasperated. "For my sanity we will switch to something simpler. Eponine! Marius! Give me 'A Little Fall of Rain.' Orchestra, prepare yourselves. And this time, the kiss."

The kiss! We've thrown around if Marius and Eponine should kiss at the end of this song or not, and up to now, we haven't. I have to kiss Jude, or *get* to kiss Jude. This may be "something simpler" to Ricardo, but this song takes every ounce of me, and I don't feel like I even have a drop left to give. And now I have to worry about the kissing thing!

Jude and I find our places and the beautiful notes begin to float through the air. I look into Jude's eyes, and I am no longer exhausted or shaken or worried about pleasing Ricardo.

"Don't you fret," I begin. My voice takes over.

Jude and I volley back and forth, taking turns with the melody and the story. Then he leans over and kisses me lightly as I fall limp in his arms.

"Bravo!" Ricardo yells. His compliments don't come easily, but I'm so aflutter from Jude's soft lips, I can barely move.

"Take five." Ricardo wipes sweat from his brow with a white

towel, and I'm brought back to reality.

We stumble to our seats where I collapse in a heap.

Jude turns around. "That rocked!" His eyebrows shoot up his forehead.

Does he mean the singing or the kiss?

"Yeah." I take a gigantic swig from my water bottle, hoping to come up with something witty to retort by the time I come up for air.

Ricardo walks past us and places a hand on each of our shoulders.

"Marvelous duet. I have been teetering on the kiss. You two simply pulled it off. Do it like that for me on show night. Yes?"

This is the first time Ricardo's cracked a smile today.

"Yes, sir." Jude smiles.

All I can do is nod.

Chapter Twenty-One

I feel the happiest I've felt in as long as I can remember. Maybe I can add something to the show. I know in my heart I actually bring something to the stage—me, Screw-up Emma, making an impact. I like that. Maybe if I work extra hard, I can change things around the house too. I've done all the laundry the last two days, braided Becca's hair, and even made all the beds this morning.

And even though I know the kiss from Jude is only because he's an incredible actor, and it's exactly the thing Marius, the gentleman, would do, I'm still tingly all over from it. That one kiss on stage was more powerful than anything Peter and I ever shared.

"Mom, when are we going back-to-school shopping?" The twins speak in a chorus. Come to think of it, I could hit Macy's pretty hard too. Natalie's Nordstrom's speech, as annoying as it was, made me realize that I was past-due for my back-to-school shopping.

"Yes, when are we going?" I smile as I bring the spaghetti I made for dinner over to the table.

Mom slides off her sandals. Her face looks pink. I see her swallow. "About shopping, girls," her voice wavers.

"Can we eat now?" Bennett asks, plopping down next to me. He's always famished.

"Put me in my chair!" Billy demands. He wants to be in the middle of everything.

"Here you go, bud." I swoop him into his high chair.

"Let's pray," Mom's voice drops to a whisper. She turns to me. "Em?"

Mom often announces who's in charge of prayers at mealtime. We're supposed to say something specific for the day, what we're worried about or thankful for. I don't want to share the things I'm thankful for — Jude, the show, Ricardo noticing my singing. And, the things I'm anxious about — Dad, Carol, Mom's drinking — probably shouldn't be aired at the kitchen table.

"God is great. God is good. Let us thank Him for this food. Amen." I smirk, and the boys dive in.

"Can I go to Build-A-Bear again this year?" Becca pipes in, remembering what she got last year when the rest of us loaded up on new jeans and sweaters.

"Me too!" Billy adds.

"I don't know how else to say this, so I'm just going to say it." Mom looks up. "Money's a little tight right now, with your dad moving out and all, so we're not going to do a big shopping trip just now."

The room is silent — a rarity in our house.

"Okay, so when?" Hannah asks, scooping spaghetti on her plate.

"I don't know exactly." Mom takes a sip of something out of her coffee mug, although it's pretty late for coffee.

"What do you mean?" I demand. I don't like where this is going.

"Maybe, when everything goes on sale. . . ." Mom's voice trails off as she cuts her spaghetti into itty bitty pieces.

"Huh?" Anna looks up.

ANGRY

"Yeah, how does Dad's moving out mean we can't get new clothes?" Hannah asks.

"He—" Mom's face twists up. "He spent some money I didn't know about, so now we don't have much left in the checkbook. We'll just have to, you know, cut back for awhile."

"What exactly did he spend money on?" I ask. Flames lick my cheeks.

Mom retaliates, "If you have a problem with it, call your dad! See if he'll take you shopping!" Mom stands up and leaves the table, taking her mug with her.

Bennett dumps a pile of parmesan on his pasta.

"Can I have s'more, pwease?" Billy asks, oblivious to the battle at hand.

"What are we going to do?" Hannah asks.

"I don't know," Anna answers. "I so need new clothes. How embarrassing to not wear something new on the first day!"

"Can I still get a teddy bear?" Becca asks, not grasping the problem.

"Me too?" Billy echoes again.

"Don't any of you get it?" I stand up. "Dad spent your clothes money." I look at the twins. "And your bear money." I look at the little ones. "On his girlfriend. There isn't a money fairy who's going to come in the middle of the night and leave the cash to get the things you want!" I turn and stamp out of the room. I'm livid. Not a single new thing for school? When was Mom going to tell us? How could Dad do this? Is he that into himself? Hello! Of course he is, or none of this would have happened. I'm only a little freaked about the clothes, though. What I really wanted was a pair of foot undies. Pristine, new dance shoes for opening night—to celebrate my role, that I've finally found something I'm good at, that Emma can do.

I slam the door to my room. The tears explode all at once like the rapid fire of machine guns. I feel like someone is piercing my heart with a spear, and with that stab all of my emotions explode. My insides ache from the stabbing. *I don't think I ask for much. I really try to help Mom out and understand the twins need things and sometimes the boys need things and sometimes Princess Becca needs things. I try to wait my turn. But this is my turn! Nothing this big has ever happened to me! I have a huge role in the school musical, and I'm not even a senior, and nobody cares! Mom never asked if I needed anything for the show! I don't know if Dad even knows I'm in the show! The only people who care at all are Ricardo and my friends.*

And Me.

Yeah, right, God! If You care so much, why is everyone in this house in such a foul mood? If You care, why isn't anyone getting their way? People love to say God has a plan for everything. All right, what's Your big plan here? Screw up my whole family's life? Well, it's working!

Knock! Knock!

"Emma, let me in!" Becca screams. I can tell she's in a snit. Well, guess what? I'm in one too.

"What?" I ask.

"You were so mean to all of us, and you made me cry, and Bennett won't say anything. Not even one word. And Billy's crying in his high chair!" She hiccups between sobs.

"Great, make me feel like a jerk because Dad's one."

"Daddy's not a jerk?" Becca tries to plead with me as I open the door, but her voice gives away her questioning.

"Yeah," I pat her head. "He is."

I hear her big sniffs behind me. "And I'm sorry I yelled," I say. She does look so broken. It makes me sad for her—for all of us. "I'm just so freakin' angry at him."

ANGRY

"Then I'm freakin' angry at him too," Becca echoes, a little less flustered.

Him who? a voice whispers.

What's that supposed to mean? I ask back.

I hear Billy whimpering and bound down the stairs to rescue him. Has Mom abandoned us too?

Chapter Twenty-Two

The first day of school I walk around in a fog. I'm not a huge fan of school. I've never done great in my classes. My favorite part of the day, by far, is lunch. I am wearing my favorite pair of jeans and a fabulous pair of enormous silver peace sign earrings I bought at an art festival this summer. Raven was sweet enough to let me borrow this really cool paisley print top. She normally wears a size or two smaller than me, but because this shirt is all loose and flowy, it works. I went into the basement and pulled out the crates that store all the clothes I've outgrown and pulled out some pretty funky T-shirts for the twins. They were actually okay with them not being brand new, because they decided none of their friends would have the same ones. We decided to call them "vintage." They were also pretty psyched to have a whole new box of clothes to fight over.

I trudge through English, Algebra, Spanish, and Chemistry. Finally the lunch bell rings! After going through the line, I find Melissa and Gracie at our usual table, unpacking their lunches. "What's up with that?" I ask. "Brown-bagging on the first day of school?" I shake my head. "Girls, very uncool." Then I remembered that Melissa brings her lunch to control what she eats so she doesn't go off the skeleton deep end again. And Gracie, the ultimate pep squad, packs hers too so Melissa won't feel stupid.

Open mouth. Insert foot.

"Your earrings are so cute!" Melissa chirps cheerily. I would have gone off on me for being so insensitive. She's so much nicer than me, letting me off the hook by changing the subject, or maybe because she avoids confrontation like the plague. Either way I feel bad.

"Thanks." I shake my head to make them sway for effect.

Raven plops down with her tray and winks. "You're lookin' sizzlin', Em."

"Apparently I got a lot of beauty sleep last night." I laugh. "Or maybe it's my stellar taste in clothes?" I smile at Raven since it is her shirt.

"So, when's the big show?" Lindsey asks as she arrives in an outfit she clearly spent a jillion dollars on and a tray brimming with French fries.

"Next week," I answer, not able to suppress the giddy bubble from rising out of my throat.

"Did that girl with the lead get her voice back?" Melissa asks, truly concerned for someone she's never met.

"Olivia's back. Something about drinking this nasty tea with vinegar in it Ricardo made her drink. She swears it was the miracle cure." I roll my eyes and shake my head until I can feel my peace signs swing back and forth to make my point. "Just the scent of vinegar makes me want to puke. Better her than me!" It sounds like I'm talking about the vinegar, but I'm really talking about the voice. I've been over-the-top careful not to strain mine. I'm paranoid that what happened to Olivia could happen to me at any second.

"I always thought the first drama production was closer to Halloween." Gracie tilts her head.

"Yeah, it usually is, but for *Les Mis*, we need a huge stage to accommodate all of the sets and stuff. So, we can't do it here." I crunch a Dorito. "We're performing at the community college, and it's only available next week. That's why I've been sweating my rear off rehearsing in the summer, because the schedule's completely whacked."

"And you're not at all excited about it?" Lindsey smiles, dipping her fry in ketchup.

"Over the top." I lean back. "I feel like standing up on the table and doing an ad."

"Go for it, girlfriend," Raven cheers.

"Rav, you shouldn't have done that." Lindsey shakes her head.

I love a dare, almost more than anything. I slide my tray closer to Lindsey's, push my chair back and use it like a stepstool to stand in the center of our circular lunch table. Hundreds of voices speak at once as our classmates hold countless discussions at their tables. Good thing I have a loud voice. "Ladies and gentlemen," I belt out like a ringmaster. There's still quite a bit of chattering going on, but a couple of people look up. "I invite you all to attend Spring Hill's production of *Les Misérables* next weekend at the community college. There are performances Friday night, Saturday night, and Saturday and Sunday matinees." Quite a few people stare at me now. "Thank you!" I end and take a bow.

My friends are howling. A few people actually clap.

"Remind me to never dare you to do anything again." Raven snorts. "Never."

"If you can do that in the cafeteria, I can't wait to see you on the real stage." Melissa smiles.

"So, should we all go Friday night and to one of the matinees?" Raven asks.

"You bet!" Lindsey smacks the table.

"I'm out Saturday. I've got violin in the morning, and Raven and I play soccer in the afternoon." Gracie says. "How about the Sunday matinee?"

"I thought you played piano." I scrunch my eyebrows at Gracie.

"Piano, violin, and flute." Gracie shrugs.

"Sunday's good by me." Melissa nods.

"Let's book it!" declares Raven.

"So, besides you . . ." Lindsey gets that mischievous look on her face. "Who should we be watching?"

"The whole show is great, really. But, have you met the new girl, Natalie? She's Cosette, and well, she's annoying as all get-out. You can throw tomatoes at her. And then there's Jude." I bat my eyelashes to make my point. "He's Marius, and he's exquisite."

"And he's behind you," Lindsey whispers, kicking me under the table.

I glance back, and there he is, with a lopsided grin. "Great commercial for the show, Emma." He laughs, his eyebrows darting up under his bangs.

"I figure we need to promote ourselves, right?" I ask. "I was just talking about how talented you are."

"Thanks." He kind of closes his eyes in acknowledgment. "Your friends are going to be blown away by your voice."

I feel my face turn Becca's favorite color—pink.

"You actually got her to shut up." Lindsey laughs.

Jude laughs too. "See you at rehearsal." He turns and tosses his trash in the nearest garbage can.

"You little vixen." Raven winks.

"It can't be all work and no play." I toss my curls and laugh. He said they'd be "blown away" by my voice!

Chapter Twenty-Three

My stomach frantically thrashes all over the place. I touch the phone application on my iPhone. I press the black circle taking me back to the main menu. I touch the phone icon again. I want my dad to come see *Les Mis*. I don't know why I want him to, but I do. I guess I want to show him what I've got, that I'm actually good at something. It might not be soccer like the twins. I might not be beautiful like Becca. I might not be a genius like Bennett or as adorable as Billy, but this is my thing. This is my moment, and I want to prove it to him. But, I wish I could tell Dad about it with ESP or that he could see an ad for it while watching ESPN. The last time I spoke with him was that dinner at Pizzaro's, which was a disaster. I feel as green as the fake apples the crew painted for props.

"All right already!" I yell at myself. I pick up the phone again, and touch his name in my contact list, before I have a chance to chicken out again.

"Hi, you've reached Will."

I exhale in relief at the recording of his voice. I don't actually have to talk to him. Huge break!

"Leave a message after the tone." He sounds like a soap opera star luring middle-aged women in with his lilting words. Gross! Is he trying to sound all sexy for Carol?

Beep!

I shake my head and force words out of my throat. "Uh, hi, Dad?" Like who else would it be? "It's Emma, and my show, I mean, *Les Misérables*, the m-m-musical for school I'm in, is next weekend. Well, like, there are shows on Friday night and S-ss-Saturday night, a week from today, actually. And then there are matinees, you know, in the afternoon on Saturday and Sunday. Anyway, I hope you can make it."

Click.

I sounded like a complete moron, stuttering and rambling like that. Well, it's done—at least half done. Now I just have to ask Mom.

It's hotter than Hades outside, and Mom turned off the air conditioner in an attempt to save money. I'm sweating through my magenta tank top, and my denim shorts are stuck to my thighs. Even though I've pulled my hair back into a ponytail, ringlets of red are plastered around my face. I grab a Mountain Dew out of the fridge. The cold can feels heavenly in my hand. I stand in front of the open refrigerator for a minute, considering how difficult it would be to cram my big old thighs onto one of the shelves. Since that's an impossible feat, I shove my head in as far as it will go and close my eyes.

I jump at something pulling my shorts. I bang my head on the roof of the fridge.

"I need to go potty!" Billy announces emphatically.

"Come on!" I scream at the throb radiating from my cranium.

"I need to go potty!" Billy repeats.

"Okay, okay," I murmur and take his hand, leading him to the bathroom.

There stands Becca blocking the door, looking lovely and cool in a rainbow-colored striped cotton sundress. "How old was I when I was born?" she asks.

"What in the world, Bec?" I rub my head where I'm sure a Fred Flintstone-sized lump is growing, and push Billy and myself past her toward the toilet.

"How old was I when I was born?"

I pull Billy's shorts and Batman undies down and set him on the potty. I contemplate the year Becca was born and how old she is now and then laugh out loud at how ridiculous her question is.

"You were zero when you were born, silly!" I ruffle her curls. "You start out at zero, and then every year after that you add a year on your birthday."

"I done!" Billy announces.

"Are you sure?" Becca eyes me suspiciously and puts her little fists on her hips.

"I *is* done!" Billy confirms, thinking Becca's questioning him.

I gather up Billy, help him wash his hands, and nod my head.

"Bec's asking me if I'm sure," I reassure him. "I know you're done going potty."

"That doesn't sound quite right," Becca puzzles.

"I'm sure." I laugh out loud and step back into the kitchen, Billy and Becca in tow. Becca slides into a fit of giggles, and I can't help giggling with her. Billy busts into the laugh fest, just so he won't be left out.

"How old was I?" he asks.

This makes all of us laugh even harder.

"What's so funny?" Mom asks as she walks in the door. She actually has a smile on her face, which I haven't seen in ages.

"I'm not so sure about her." Becca giggles pointing to me.

"And, I'm not so sure about you, missy!" I reach out and tickle her.

Billy reaches out with wiggly fingers in attempt to tickle us all.

"It's nice to see you laughing," Mom says, fanning herself with the mail. Seeing her fanning herself reminds me of people in an audience fanning themselves with programs, and I remember what I need to ask her. Everyone's so happy, this might just go okay.

"Hey, Mom."

"Hey, what?"

"You know I've been practicing for *Les Mis*."

"It does seem to have consumed a bit of your time." She pulls two ice cubes out of the freezer and clunks them into a wine glass. "Like every day." She winks at me. It's so weird. Mom smiling. Becca and Billy and I laughing. These are normal things, or at least they're supposed to be normal things, but lately the only things that have been standard around here have been tears and fights and whining. It's such an unspoken relief to be joking and winking and tickling.

"Yeah, well, the performances are next weekend, and I know you have to work and stuff, but will you come?"

Mom stops pouring the Chardonnay into her glass and sets down the bottle. "Of course, I'll come, Em."

"Me too! Me too!" Becca jumps up and down.

"Me too! Me too!" Billy jumps up and down with her.

"Don't leave us out." The twins say in unison as they stroll in from the back where they've been passing the soccer ball. Bennett is two steps after them. He looks straight at Mom and declares, "I want to see Emma sing."

"That settles it." Mom laughs. "You're going to have a big cheering section, Em."

I feel a rush of warmth inside, like when the curtain first rises, allowing the audience and the cast to see each other for the first time. There's a relief, but also anticipation. The hard part, the

ANGRY

meeting, is over; but the even harder part, the giving the audience what they came for part, is just beginning.

I wonder if Dad will be part of that audience. And, if he does come, will he hide in the corner or sit on the fringe of the family, like next to Bennett or something? Or maybe, just maybe, the beautiful love story will wrap itself around him and Mom, and they'll see what jerks they've been and get back together. Or, no freakin' way, he wouldn't bring Carol! Would he?

Chapter Twenty-Four

It's "Hell Week." I know most people dread this week—packed with grueling rehearsals until all hours of the night—but I live for this week. There's something about being completely immersed in the theatre and the practice and the exhaustion that I love! Does that mean I'm a masochist? Or maybe this isn't hell to me compared to what's been going on at home. I wake up at dawn each morning and go to school. After school Kate and I go to McDonald's or Taco Bell, depending on the day, grab food, and then drive over to the community college. I have my bag permanently stashed in the backseat with all my makeup and shoes and junk. And then, we rehearse, for hours.

We get to wear full makeup and costumes for rehearsals this week. It seals the deal for me, completely transforming me into Eponine. I am Emma no more.

"Tonight we will be going through the entire show from the first note to the last. Just like the real thing. No interruptions, from me, or from anyone else. If the orchestra decides to play "Zippidy Doo Da," you keep singing. If your cast mates forget their lines, try to prompt them, and if that doesn't work, say their lines for them and go on." Ricardo smiles wryly. He's notorious for stopping scenes part-way through and interrupting solos mid-note.

I tingle from my toes strapped into my character shoes all the way to my scalp where bobby pins hold in Eponine's signature floppy hat.

"While you are not on stage, I urge you to watch the performance. This is your only chance to see the show you are in. Take notes. Learn from the rest of the cast. This is it. Places everyone!" Ricardo rolls the *r* in *everyone*.

There's shuffling of feet, flickering of lights, fluttering of curtains. People scurry to places on stage. All the guys are in the opening number. The Xs in tape have been removed. By now, they are etched into our minds.

Layers of skirts swish around Kate's long legs. She grabs my hand and gives it a squeeze. I feel her pulse racing. The moment is too perfect to speak. It's so real, I almost forget we are high school girls singing and dancing. I follow her to the third row aisle. There is silence. Then the conductor taps his stick on his music stand.

In the smothering silence, the curtains open as if in slow motion. In an instant the stage comes to life, like Snow White when the prince's kiss wakes her from her slumber. The lights turn on, the trumpets blow, voices fill the auditorium.

I'm riveted to the stage where Patrick portrays Jean Valjean, a poor man imprisoned for stealing food for his family to eat. He escapes jail. A bishop, played by Keegan, a super-tall freshman with an outrageously awesome voice, takes him in. On the run, Jean Valjean steals from the bishop. Desperate men do desperate things.

"Props! Where are the silver candlesticks?" Ricardo barks. "Good cover-up, Jean!"

The police catch Jean and return him to the bishop's home. The bishop claims he gave Jean Valjean the silver as a gift. The bishop stuffs Jean Valjean's bags with the rest of his valuables, and as Jean Valjean looks at him with disbelief, the bishop asks him to pay this kindness forward. He sings, "To love another person is to see the face of God."

I'm weeping. Tears stream down my face. I've heard them practice this a hundred times in rehearsals, but parts of it, just Keegan singing, or Patrick running, or Ricardo interrupting, or the orchestra restarting, or I'm doing my homework, or talking to Kate, or texting Lindsey, but never have I given it my full attention.

Much like God lately. He's been talking to me, but I haven't really paid attention. I've brushed Him off and pushed Him away and haven't taken the time to sit down and listen.

Now, I feel God singing to me through Keegan's voice. He is here with me and this time He wants my full attention. I can't escape, and actually, I don't know if I want to run anymore.

I love you that much, Emma—as pure as the bishop loved Jean Valjean. The bishop doesn't care about Jean Valjean's past, but trusts him to make the right choices in the future. Same with us. I don't care what you've done. We're going to start right here, right now. I will give you the gifts to help you get to the next place—not silver, but what you need, and I will trust you to do what's right. Don't worry; you'll make some mistakes. But I'll help you get back up when you fall. All I ask in return is that you love Me.

Kate taps my knee and rushes off to get in place for the next song. I don't think she noticed my sopping cheeks and smeary eyes. Thankfully I don't go on until the second act. I slip off to the bathroom and wash my face. I'm thankful for a break in my heavy thinking. It's a bit too much to swallow. Am I really ready for everything God was saying? Do I buy into it all? Plus, this really isn't the best time for a heart to heart with God.

That's what you think.

Nice try, God. I shake His voice from my brain. The cold water clears my reverie.

But, back in my seat the story continues to unfold, and so does my conversation with God. I know the story of *Les Mis* by heart, and I cry every time I see it. But maybe I knew it too well, like a song when you know all the words and you stop paying attention to what you're even singing. I feel like I'm watching *Les Mis* for the first time, and like I'm understanding what Jesus did for me for the first time too.

Jean Valjean begins a new life. He stays true to his promise to the bishop and takes in Fantine, a young woman driven to prostitution to earn money to care for her daughter. Fantine dies, but Jean Valjean promises he will care for her child, and so the cycle of selfless love continues. He gives up life as he knows it to care for this little girl.

I gave My life for you, Emma.

Warm tears spill from my eyes all over again.

Of course You did. I've known it all along. I can't stay out of this conversation any longer. It's time I talk to God for real. *I never doubted that You were real or that You died for me, Jesus. I just didn't think about what that meant, or realize how much You cared. I see it now through the show. I can be so dense. I've been living and breathing this show, and it takes the dress rehearsal for me to see. Lately, I've felt like nobody loves me. I used to think my mom did. I used to think my dad did. But, now I'm not so sure. I thought they loved each other, too, but they don't. I don't know if they even know what love is. I'm not sure if I do either. My friends are great. I mean they support me and listen to me, but they don't really get me. They can't understand what it's like every day. They don't know what it's like to be me. I've felt so empty and so alone.*

God reads right into my soul and tells me the words I need to hear most. *But I know. I'm there with you every day. I see it all. And, don't forget, Emma, I made you. I know exactly what it's like to be you. And as far as knowing what love is, I am love.*

Chapter Twenty-Five

I've lost track of time in this dark theatre. Out of the corner of my eye, I catch Kate darting in and out of her seat. The chorus is on stage more than anyone else, and she has costume changes for all the different scenes. She whispers something to me once or twice. I think I mumble something back. But now it's the second act, and Cosette is all grown-up and singing in her pretty white dress on stage.

"Ai yai yai!" I rub my forehead. That means I'm supposed to be in the wings! I only have a song and a half until I'm on!

I fly to the dressing room, which is way cool. At school the girls use the band room and the boys use the choir room to change. We tape black paper over the windows so no one can see in, and we just run around in our bras and set up our makeup kits on the floor. Here I have my own chair with a vanity and a mirror. My makeup bag waits for me. I retouch the best I can. As I swipe charcoal across my lids, Jesse from the crew calls out, "Marius, Eponine, you're up!"

I tuck a bobby pin through a hunk of copper curls to secure my cap and rush out to the wings.

Natalie and Patrick are just finishing the notes of their duet. I take a deep breath and find my place on stage. I know this freakin' cap is going to slip off, and I'm on for the next four songs!

This is not how I do things! Well, it's how I do everything else in my life, but this is not how I do theatre. Everything else can be haphazard and rushed and half-cocked, but when I perform I like my costume and my makeup to be perfect. Maybe I should stop being haphazard about God too.

Good idea.

Funny, God, but not now.

I wanted to sit and really get into character. To run over the blocking, where I position my body on stage, and the most important notes I have to hit, but not this time. This time, I just have to wing it. Here goes . . .

"In my life," I sing.

"Louder, Eponine," Ricardo coaches.

I get through every line and dance by sheer willpower, okay, plus I've practiced so much I could probably get through this whole show in my sleep. I only have one quick break over the next six songs. The rest is mostly me singing solos and interacting with Jude. When I'm done, I collapse in a seat in the back and retrace my performance in my head until the finale. I'm furious at myself for not being on. I bang my feet on the floor as I reconstruct my moments on stage. My cap did fall off. My voice was flat on a couple of notes. And I don't even remember if I got all the lines right. I think I might have repeated one of the verses twice and skipped another one altogether. The more I think about it, the harder my tongue pushes against my teeth. It's applying so much pressure they might pop out of my mouth.

The finale! Back up on stage!

Calm down, Emma. Our conversation was worth a little distraction tonight. Tomorrow's the real deal. You'll shine then.

Goosebumps spread from my freckled shoulders down my arms. Despite my funk, a smile spreads across my lips. I sing the

ANGRY

final song with the rest of the cast and bow.

"Okay, people! That's a wrap!" Ricardo's voice booms. The house lights go on and an audible sigh fills the auditorium.

"Gather round for debriefing." An audible moan fills the auditorium.

Ricardo proceeds to read off every error he's noted during our performance. Mixed in, of course are all of my screwups. Hearing them announced in front of the whole cast is like rubbing salt into my wounds. It feels like Ricardo will never get to the end of comments scrawled in his yellow legal pad. Finally, he exhales, stands up and announces, "Tomorrow night we meet again. Between now and then make sure you eat and sleep!"

Driving home, I roll down the windows.

Kate turns off my stereo. "Do you mind?" she asks. "I'm just too jumpy."

"Sure." I shrug. I'm not very chatty. I keep trying to run over my mistakes in my head, but everything God said is swirling around, and it's hard to focus.

"I don't know if I'll sleep at all tonight." Kate puts her hand on my arm.

"I'm going to crash." I shake my head. I feel completely zapped.

She nods. We pull into her driveway.

"Thanks, Emma." She starts to get out of the car, and then pops her head back in, "The show is tomorrow!" she screams.

"Crazy." I laugh.

The warm night air smells sweet as it blows on my face, lulling me down from my adrenaline high. The world is quiet. My pulse gradually returns to a normal rate. I loosen my grip on the steering wheel. It's a clean slate tomorrow, right? God said I get to start fresh; I hope He's referring to my performance.

It's late when I get home. A hush has fallen over the house. Even Mom seems to have gone to bed. For the first time in, well, in as long as I can remember, I feel at peace. The house is a lovely quiet. A slight breeze blows through the windows. We're still not splurging for AC, despite the August heat, but tonight that doesn't aggravate me.

I sling my sacks on the counter and do a quick emptying and refilling. I grab Pop-Tarts and Doritos and a couple of Mountain Dews from the cupboards and cram them into my school bag and my show bag to get me through whatever comes tomorrow.

Tomorrow I'll have to fake my way through class. I clearly didn't do any homework. I'm screwed in English first period. I guess I can scrawl some math problems during English and look over my Spanish vocab in Math. In Chemistry we're doing a lab, so I'm counting on Gracie, who is my lab partner, to have read the chapter. I have Family Solutions right after lunch and can do the worksheet for History then. Whatever. It's all good. And then, our performance. *Ummmm*, just the thought of it gives me a happy buzz.

There's a heap of dinner dishes piled on the counter. I rinse and load them into the dishwasher, which is filthy and packed! This kind of thing usually drives me crazy. It's so nice to be relaxed for once. I squirt in the dishwashing liquid. Shut the door and push Run.

The dishwasher hums a tranquil tune. I waltz upstairs to the rhythm of the water swishing over dishes and drift off to sleep.

Chapter Twenty-Six

So, today is the day—the day of the performance. It doesn't seem right that we have school today. I assume I went to my classes and ate lunch with my friends, but I really don't remember any of it. I floated through my schedule like the Phantom of the Opera floated in the basement of the old opera house unnoticed. Only I don't remember the Phantom being highly caffeinated.

Tonight I will do everything perfectly. Last night was a shaky warm-up, but you know what? It was completely the right thing. Seeing that first half and talking with God. That was what I really needed. *God, I feel so much more peaceful today. Knowing You are with me means everything. I know I can nail it up there, and somehow, if I can do that, I feel like everything will be better.*

I'm always with You.

His answers are funny sometimes—like, *Duh, Emma, of course you feel more peaceful when you actually talk to Me.* Only God would never say it like that, but I get the point. I need to rely more on Him.

You've got it.

I smile and fast-forward to tonight.

I'll spend the whole first act making sure my makeup's perfect and getting into character and warming up my voice. Then, when I go on in the second act, I'll nail it! Everyone's going to be there tonight to see me: Lindsey, Raven, Gracie, and Melissa, Mom, Becca, Hannah, Anna, Bennett, and even little Billy. Well, everyone but Dad. He sent a one-liner text:

`Sorry, would love to see you, but I have a business dinner I cannot miss.`

So clean and easy for him. He didn't have the guts to actually tell me, just texted it like he was checking another item off his list. At first it hit me like the mugger beating up Tom Collins in the first act of *Rent*. But honestly, I've pushed it somewhere far away, somewhere I can pull it out later and deal with it. I'm not going to let Dad worry me now. I'm not going to let anything worry me now. This is my moment.

/ / /

I stand in the wings entranced by Natalie's voice. For as much as she bugs the crap out of me on any given day, her rendition of Cosette is flawless. I morph from Emma into my character, Eponine. And Eponine is so jealous of that beautiful creature who has captured Marius's heart. Doesn't she know *I* love him? I've always loved him. But still, she's so pretty and dainty, and I'm so dirty and grimy, both literally and figuratively, from the poor, tough life on the streets I live.

I slink into my position on stage unnoticed by the audience as their eyes are glued to Cosette. I sing my first notes. They pierce the air. My voice is so different from Cosette's. Hers is high and delicate. Mine is full of emotion.

The songs flow. I hit each note. I am Eponine. My heart aches with her pain. As I sing the songs that stab my soul, they cut through the auditorium and fill the air with pain and relief and truth and love. I'm no longer singing to Marius or to an audience but to God. "And You will keep me safe." Tears stream down my face as I die a gentle death in Marius's arms. Then, Jude's lips brush mine.

I spend the next eight numbers in the dressing room until the finale. It's crazy in here. Everyone is stripping off dresses and throwing on new ones for the wedding scene. Petticoats fly everywhere!

"Wow, Emma!" Kate hugs me so tight I fear the seams in my dress might pop. "You totally nailed it out there! I mean, I thought you were Eponine."

"Yeah, I'm glad I didn't have any time on stage with you," Olivia pipes in. "You totally stole the show!"

"Hardly." I wink, but inside I'm eating this up. It feels awesome to have people think I'm good at something for once.

I chug a huge bottle of water and check my makeup and re-pin my cap while chatting with the other girls who are in between scenes.

I'm helping Kate with her zipper when Natalie swooshes by in a wedding dress.

"Like, you were so fab, Emma. I'm such an excellent judge of talent, and you've got it." Natalie looks down at herself and pushes her breasts up, so they peek out of her dress a bit. "Now, how do I look?"

"Great." I grin. I refrain from turning the spotlight back to me. Getting Natalie to compliment someone other than herself is a major accomplishment.

"I do, don't I? Poor Jude is done for." She blows Kate and me a kiss and scuttles back to the stage.

Kate bursts out laughing and gives me a hug. "You really were amazing, Em."

"I felt good out there," I confess.

As Kate dashes away I call to her, "Break a leg."

"Thanks," her voice trails down the corridor.

After the show there's a flurry outside the dressing room doors. Family members and friends flock to give well-wishes and flowers. Lindsey grabs my arm and pushes her mouth against my ear, so I can hear her over the crowd, "You were amazing!" She pulls me to the side where Gracie, Melissa, and Raven all wait for me with a sign, "Emma Rocks!" and a huge bouquet of pink roses.

They all hug me, and they're jumping up and down and taking pictures. I feel like a celebrity on the red carpet.

"Way to go, girl!" Raven flashes her gorgeous white teeth.

"You're really talented." Gracie strokes my arm in genuine adoration.

"Emma, I knew you could sing. I mean anytime you sing anything, even 'Happy Birthday' or to the radio or something, it sounds so beautiful. But, you made me cry." Tears linger in Melissa's eyes.

Tears well up in my own eyes.

I've been so down on myself and so hungry for attention. I wanted people to notice me—to love me. I acted so over-the-top dramatic with my friends and ran around with Peter, playing the bad girl, trying to fill the gaps in my heart, to make people notice me. But that was for all the wrong reasons. People are noticing me now. But they're noticing me for who I am, someone with an abundance of emotion and a passion for the theatre, which is such a healthier outlet for all these feelings that rage around inside of me. To tap into my emotions on stage makes the most of my talent instead of throwing my feelings around recklessly, not caring where they fall or who they hurt.

Now that Eponine is dead, my anger dies with her. I know that the storm of my life—my parents' divorce and their hate and dishonesty and instability—is clearing. Now that I've turned it over to God, I don't need to cling to the pain and the anger as a way to understand everything. I know God is with me. Not just to get me through the pangs of the divorce, but to help me out of all of the crap I've been wallowing in.

I look around at my circle of friends. They do love me, even if they don't understand me. Something slams my legs. I'm caught off guard and lose my balance a little. I look down to see Billy hugging my knees.

"Billy." I laugh and scoop him up. Behind Raven are the twins, Becca, Bennett, and Mom.

"I am so honored to be your mother," Mom says in the steadiest voice she's had in months. I feel a lump the size of the princess's golden ball in *The Frog Prince* form in my heart. It tries to escape my mouth, but gets stuck in my throat on the way up. I quiver as the tears that took root with Melissa's compliment grow and spill down my face. My friends part to make room for Mom, who holds me close enough I can feel her heart beating against my chest. Bennett and Hannah and Anna and little Becca join in, so we're all in one big family hug. Dad's not here, but I sense we'll be okay without him. As we cling to each other, red hair and freckles everywhere, I feel entwined in love. And then, a warm golden feeling fills all the empty spaces between our jagged elbows and crooked knees, and I know that it is God, filling all the spaces we cannot fill by ourselves.

About the Author

Laura L. Smith is the author of *Skinny* and *Hot*. She believes in God. She believes in true love. She believes in fairies. She believes if she bangs hard enough on the back of her wardrobe she will get to Narnia, someday. She believes eating chocolate is good for you. She believes part of her soul lives in France, part of it at the beach, and part of it in Oxford, Ohio, where she lives with her husband and four children, because when she goes to those places she feels at home, as if she's always belonged. She believes heaven will be much the same. She believes that God created her to be the mother of her children and to write the stories He wanted to tell. *Angry* is the third of these stories. She has seen *Les Misérables* three times and sobbed every time. Visit her website at www.laurasmithauthor.com.

Read Laura L. Smith's first two TH1NK novels!

Skinny
Laura L. Smith
Teen Melissa Rollins is determined to have the perfect body, even if it makes her throw up. Whether you're a young woman, a mom, or a youth pastor, you'll appreciate the truth and compassion in Melissa's struggle with anorexia. Will she hear God's voice before it's too late?
978-1-60006-356-5

Hot
Laura L. Smith
Lindsey is gorgeous and dresses like a model, but inside she feels alone. She feels as though no one truly understands her—until she meets Noah. Noah possesses a calm self-confidence that Lindsey craves. But what price will she pay to escape to the comfort of Noah's soft words and strong arms?
978-1-60006-622-1

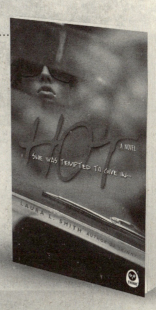

To order copies, call NavPress at **1-800-366-7788** or log on to **www.NavPress.com**.

NAVPRESS
Discipleship Inside Out™